Hands shaking, Morgan closed her eyes as she careened backward, heart pounding, praying she wouldn't end up as a warning story on the news.

In the end, though, the sedan's back end came to rest gently against the trunk of a huge pine tree while the front half of the car climbed crookedly up toward the road like a drunken college student after a bender.

Lord help her. She hadn't even been here an hour and things were already going downhill. Literally.

After a quick full-body shake to disperse some excess adrenaline and make sure she wasn't injured, Morgan set about figuring out how to get unstuck from her current situation. Her train of thought was quickly derailed, however, by the passenger door flying open. Stunned, she stared wide-eyed at the last person she'd ever expected to see again.

Ely.

No last name. They'd never exchanged them. The one-night stand she'd never forgotten.

Not even after ten years.

Dear Reader,

This story takes place on Whidbey Island, a quaint place off the coast of Washington State that's filled with rolling farms and scenic coastlines and a thriving arts culture. When I sat down to think about new stories, where I wanted to set them, this location just called to me. Then Ely and Morgan came along, with their backstories and their passions, and this book was born. Oh, and I decided to set the story in October so we could have the big costume ball at Halloween! (Because who doesn't love characters who dress up as pirates and mermaids and space droids, right?)

I do hope you'll enjoy reading about Ely and Morgan's journey to love and the bumps along the way. Their story was a pleasure to write, and who knows—maybe someday I'll get to visit the wonderful Whidbey Island myself!

Until next time, happy reading!

Traci <3

ISLAND REUNION WITH THE SINGLE DAD

TRACI DOUGLASS

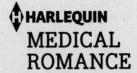

HARLEQUIN
MEDICAL
ROMANCE

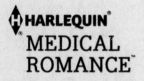

HARLEQUIN®
MEDICAL
ROMANCE™

Recycling programs
for this product may
not exist in your area.

ISBN-13: 978-1-335-40924-9

Island Reunion with the Single Dad

Copyright © 2022 by Traci Douglass

For questions and comments about the quality of this book, please contact us at CustomerService@Harlequin.com.

Harlequin Enterprises ULC
22 Adelaide St. West, 41st Floor
Toronto, Ontario M5H 4E3, Canada
www.Harlequin.com

Printed in U.S.A.

Traci Douglass is a *USA TODAY* bestselling romance author with Harlequin, Entangled Publishing and Tule Publishing, and has an MFA in Writing Popular Fiction from Seton Hill University. She writes sometimes funny, usually awkward, always emotional stories about strong, quirky, wounded characters overcoming past adversity to find their forever person. Heartfelt, healing happily-ever-afters. Connect with her through her website: tracidouglassbooks.com.

Books by Traci Douglass

Harlequin Medical Romance

First Response in Florida

The Vet's Unexpected Hero
Her One-Night Secret

One Night with the Army Doc
Finding Her Forever Family
A Mistletoe Kiss for the Single Dad
A Weekend with Her Fake Fiancé
Their Hot Hawaiian Fling
Neurosurgeon's Christmas to Remember
Costa Rican Fling with the Doc

Visit the Author Profile page
at Harlequin.com for more titles.

To Princess Clara,

See you across the rainbow bridge.
Love and miss you, missy poo. <3

And to my Zoom Writing Cohort:

Thank you Aleks, Carol and Lucy
for all the words and support and wonderful chats.

Couldn't have gotten through this without you!

CHAPTER ONE

WELCOME TO WHIDBEY ISLAND...

Dr. Morgan Salas stared at the large wooden sign near the pebbled beach, with its carved twin eagles and painted seascape, an image of the car ferry she'd just departed across the bottom. She took a deep breath of fresh Pacific Northwest air drifting through the window of the sedan, the late-September air crisp with the scents of fallen leaves and recent rainfall. For the first time in recent memory, she felt...happy. Lighter. More hopeful. Maybe she could find some measure of the peace and contentment she'd lost when Ben died. She had a month here. Perhaps it would be enough.

She'd enjoyed the trip from Mukilteo, Washington, on the mainland to the tiny, quaint coastal town of Clinton on the island. She'd had twenty minutes on the ferry to just enjoy the scenery and leave her cares behind.

Hopefully. Maybe. Okay, probably not, but she was working on it.

From what she'd researched online, Whidbey Island was known for its "reserved individuality" and "effortless ease." She prayed some of that ease would rub off on her while she was here. First, though, now that she was on dry land again, she had to get to her appointment on the other side of the island near Freeland.

Morgan checked out the open window of her rented sedan for oncoming traffic on the two-lane asphalt ahead, then managed to get around a few slower-moving cars until she was on the open roadway again. Cool wind in her hair, she passed several signs as she headed out of Clinton for the Scenic Isle Way, part of the Cascade Loop and the only section entirely contained within an island. She'd read about that, too, being something of a fact geek. The views here were gorgeous, no doubt. The knot between her shoulder blades and a bit more of her old anger and grief drifted away. And sure, maybe the roads here were bit narrow and...whoa! Those hairpin turns seemed to come out of nowhere, but it was all good. She'd take it slow and steady. That always won the race, right?

Well, usually. Unless someone cheated. Like Ben did.

Her pulse kicked a notch higher as she glanced at the clock in the dashboard. Twenty minutes.

She could still make it on time, barring any more holdups. She hated being late.

Except just ahead, traffic had slowed again. *Dammit.* Morgan slowed, then leaned out the window, craning her neck to see the problem. It was the middle of nowhere, farm fields bordered by forest on either side. But a slight incline ahead kept her from seeing beyond it. Huh. In the distance, animals grazed, and she spotted a few tourists gawking and taking pictures.

What could possibly be out here to cause such a ruckus?

Ugh. Morgan did not have time for this. Not today, anyway. So, after checking again for oncoming traffic, she nosed out of line into the opposite lane then hurried up the incline, thinking she'd bypass the crowd. Except when she got to the top of the hill, all she saw was sheep. Sheep everywhere. Including a big one square in her lane.

Alarmed, Morgan slammed on the brakes, only to have her back tires fishtail off the still-wet asphalt. *Crap.* Silence thudded loud in her ears as the sheep in front of her watched impassively, chewing its cud. Cursing, Morgan tapped her accelerator, hoping to nudge all four tires back onto the roadway. Except that, coupled with the slick and muddy berm, only made her slide farther into the ditch. Hands shaking, she closed her eyes as she careened backward, heart pounding, praying she wouldn't end up as a warning story on the news. *Woman illegally passes traffic, ends up trapped and dead beneath a ton of flipped steel.* Kids, don't try this at home.

In the end, though, the sedan's back end came to rest gently against the trunk of a huge pine tree while the front half of the car climbed crookedly up toward the road like a drunken college coed after a bender.

Lord, help her. She hadn't even been here an hour and things were already going downhill. Literally.

After a quick full-body shake to disperse some excess adrenaline and make sure she wasn't injured, Morgan set about figuring out how to get unstuck from her current situation. Her train of thought was quickly derailed, however, by the passenger door flying open. Stunned, she stared wide-eyed at the last person she'd ever expected to see again.

Ely.

No last name. They'd never exchanged them. The one-night stand she'd never forgotten.

Not even after ten years.

"Are you okay?" he asked, cutting through her befuddled thoughts.

"Uh…" Morgan frowned.

Am I okay? Maybe I hit my head after all, and this is all a hallucination.

She took a deep breath and gave a small prayer of thanks that at least he didn't seem to recognize her. "Uh…yes. I think I'm—"

"Hang on a minute and let me check you over." Before she could finish, he'd reached over from the passenger side to run his hands over her arms and legs, checking for injury, but that only made her scalp tingle more.

"Stop. Please!" Out of sorts and far too aware of his hands on her body, she pulled away, heat prickling her cheeks. "I'm fine. Just a little shaken. Thank you."

Her voice trembled, to her eternal mortification. This was ridiculous. Ely was just a man. A man she'd had sex with, once upon a time. Also, a man who obviously didn't even remember her anyway. She was making a huge deal out of nothing. He shouldn't affect her like this. She obviously didn't affect him at all. Ely didn't seem to care in the least.

Well, other than the fact he was trying to get her out of her predicament. Okay. Fine. That part was helpful. She peered past his broad shoulder toward the crest of the ditch, where the same tourists who'd been photographing the sheep were now snapping pictures of her. Perfect. Exactly how she wanted to start her monthlong stint on the island. As a photo op. Morgan cleared her throat and fiddled with her horribly wrinkled shirt to avoid looking at him. "Did anyone else slide off the road?"

"Nope," Ely said, his tone a bit curt now, his expression clearly irritated. He leaned back, muscled arms braced on the door frame, filling the space like he had a right to, sucking up all her oxygen. He shrugged, then narrowed his gaze on her. "Probably because no one else was driving like a maniac. These roads get very slick after a rain. You could've killed yourself or someone else pulling a stunt like that."

Her hackles rose, her chest tight. "First of all, I'm not a maniac. I have an important meeting to get to. And second, doesn't it rain all the time in the Pacific Northwest? That's kind of what you're known for it, isn't it?"

She forced herself to inhale. Arguing with him wouldn't get her out of this any sooner, and she couldn't risk missing her appointment. Time to end this here and now. And if that meant swallowing her pride, fine. "Sorry. You're right." She bit her tongue and forced a smile. "I wasn't thinking. Can you help me get out of here, please?"

"Of course." His voice and expression softened, and her heart did a weird little flip. *Damn.* He looked so much like she remembered. Dark and handsome and windswept, his smile revealing dimples in his cheeks. Lord, she'd forgotten the devastating effect those dimples had on her common sense. Ely hiked his chin toward the door behind her and said, "Hop out and I'll see if I can't get you steered back onto the road."

Still dazed and shaky, Morgan undid her seat belt and opened the driver's side door. Stepped out on wobbly knees, only to find her new shoes stuck in mud almost up to her ankles. Before she could despair too much, Ely was beside her, his tawny gaze twinkling as he tried, and failed, to keep his smile from growing into a full-blown grin.

"Go on and help her out, Ely!" someone shouted from up top.

"Put those capable hands of yours to good use, Doc!" another guy yelled.

Blood whooshed in her ears, and Morgan

wondered if it was possible to die from embarrassment. Because it certainly felt like she could, especially when Ely grabbed her around the waist and lifted her into his arms. A sucking sound echoed as her feet popped free of the muck, but all she could focus on was the feel of his hard chest against her, the heat of him through her clothes, his clean scent of soap and sandalwood. She'd forgotten how tall he was, a good foot above her own five-four. Strong, too. An unwanted shock of desire curled her toes inside her ruined pumps, and Morgan pushed hard against him. "Put me down, please."

He walked a few feet over to a grassy area and did as she asked. Their gazes locked and time slowed as the years drifted away. Suddenly they were back on a beach on this very island. Two young, stupid college kids living like there was no tomorrow.

Except life had taught her too well that there was always a day after.

"Sorry." She looked away, not sure why she was apologizing. Her stomach clenched, even though she'd done nothing wrong. Neither had he. Ely blinked down at her a beat or two, then took her hand to silently lead her up the side of the ditch to the berm. People clapped as they emerged at the summit, and she tried to look less discombobulated than she felt.

Morgan hated unwanted attention. The glare of the spotlight. The constant searing scald of gossip. She'd gotten more than enough of that after Ben's funeral. The whispers behind her back from the staff at the hospital. Conversations ending abruptly whenever she appeared.

Even though rationally she knew this was different, it felt all too similar. Moving stiffly, she sidled off to the side as Ely went back down into the ditch to gun the sedan's engine, sending a spray of mud flying as he zoomed the car back up onto the roadway. The crowd finally dispersed.

He left the engine running and walked back to Morgan, stopping a foot or so away from her.

"You've got…" he said, frowning.

"What?" Scowling, Morgan self-consciously wiped her cheek.

"No. The other side. Here." Ely tipped her chin up with a finger, then swiped his thumb across her jaw. Her lungs tightened and she thought she might pass out, completing her humiliation. Her skin still tingled even after he let her go. "There. Gone. Just a speck of mud."

"Oh…" she mumbled, touching the spot, nearly drowning in his eyes before pulling herself to safety. Flustered, she smoothed her hands down the front of her pantsuit to make sure nothing else was stained or missing. Yep. She must've hit her head and knocked something loose. Like her common sense.

Doing her best to regain her composure, Morgan stepped away and gave him her most polite smile, the one that appeased even her most irascible patients. "Thank you so much for your help. Now I need to go. Please excuse me."

Gah!

Unfortunately, Morgan had no idea how to greet an old one-night stand. Probably because she'd thought she'd never see him again. He'd never called afterward, even though she'd given him her number, so obviously he hadn't been interested.

Things had changed so much. *She* had changed so much.

"No problem," Ely called after her as she walked back to her sedan. "Take it easy on these roads. Next time you might not be so lucky, and I won't be there to help."

Feeling like a five-year-old who'd gotten caught eating paste, she climbed into the car and resisted thunking her forehead on the steering wheel. *Good Lord.* The last thing she needed right now was driving advice from the guy she'd banged on the beach a decade prior.

As calmly as possible, Morgan refastened her seat belt, checked her mirrors, then started down the road again with her hands at ten and two. She needed to focus on her meeting and not on the gorgeous man from her past, who was growing smaller by the second in her rearview mirror.

Dr. Elyas Malik stood there along the roadside, watching Morgan's car drive away, still a bit flummoxed. Who'd have thought helping a farmer herd his sheep off the roadway would lead to an unexpected reunion with the one girl he'd never quite forgotten?

Morgan.

After getting back into his old truck, Ely headed for home to change his clothes before he returned to the clinic. About a mile down the main road, he signaled, then turned off onto a winding lane that led through the countryside surrounding Wingate. The huge compound had belonged to his parents, his father's pride and joy. It was nothing like Ely would ever have bought for himself, though. But after the plane crash, he and his brother, Sam, had inherited his father's tech empire and everything that went with it. And while Ely had still pursued his dreams of becoming a doctor, his little brother, Sam, had chosen to take over the family business. Ely stayed at Wingate and Sam lived mainly in New York City, though he came back a few times a year to visit.

Most days, he didn't think about the money. It was just a part of him. He was privileged and he knew it, and he did his best to always give back to others, both in his work and his life. But today, Wingate, his vast, sustainable home, was at the top of his mind, probably because the anniversary of his parents' deaths was coming up next month. In fact, the internet was already awash with old photos of Ely's parents and the rise of the techno-titan his father had become.

He still missed them, even after all these years, and because of them and what had happened to them when he'd been just eighteen, family was the most important thing for him. He was happy here on Whidbey Island, living his little, private life, with his son, Dylan. And yes, his own ill-fated marriage hadn't worked out, but he'd gotten full custody after his divorce, mainly because his ex-wife, Raina, traveled so much for her job as a successful supermodel, and they both wanted

Dylan to have some stability in his life. So, Ely's main goal in life was to be present for his son. Sunday dinners, the holidays and the warm, fuzzy nights playing board games by the fire. But unfortunately, he was also a busy doctor with a thriving practice.

He made another turn and pulled up to the keypad near the metal gates at the entrance. Punched in his code, then waited while the gates slid open before heading up the steep drive to the house. Modern architecture full of steel and glass sparkled in the hazy sunshine. Gardens and greenhouses and several experimental labs sprawled around the main residence, generating sustainable crops grown only with water and air. It all fit right in with the Whidbey Island vibe.

Every day, Ely was reminded of the great man his father had been, and how he'd failed to live up to his father's lofty ideals. Every day, Ely vowed to do better. For himself. For Dylan. There were many things money couldn't buy, and he knew that better than most.

He hurried inside to change his clothes then get back to work, where his colleague Dr. Gregory Anderson was waiting to introduce Ely to his new temporary partner for the month of October while Dr. Greg and his wife took a much-needed and well-deserved vacation to Australia.

"Ely," Mrs. MacIntosh, his housekeeper, called up to him when he was halfway up the stairs. "Is that you?"

"Yes. Why? In kind of a rush," Ely called as he continued to his rooms on the second floor. In his bedroom, he quickly stripped off his mud-splattered shirt and dress pants before hopping in the shower. After a quick scrub, he pulled on a fresh pair of pants, plus a shirt and tie. Smoothed a hand through his dark hair that always had a mind of its own, a flash of memory rushing through his mind, making his breath catch.

Morgan. Their night on the beach, bathed in starlight and nothing else. They'd both been so young then, so naive. The world had changed now. For him, at least.

He swallowed hard, pushing those memories away. No. Life marched onward. You either went with it, got out of the way or got run over by it. And Ely was determined never to be roadkill again.

CHAPTER TWO

MORGAN PULLED INTO the clinic parking lot at six fifteen and sighed. The place looked brand-new, due to a recent remodel Dr. Greg had mentioned. Squaring her shoulders, she changed her shoes, then took a deep breath and headed inside to where Dr. Greg waited for her in the reception area, looking the same as he always had—like an older Cary Grant. Same twinkling eyes, same square-jawed handsomeness, same tall, elegant frame.

"Morgan, my dear." He enveloped her in a big hug. "I was worried. The ferry company told me they'd arrived right on time. Was the traffic bad?"

"Sort of." No way was she telling him about the ditch incident with Ely. She returned his hug, then pulled back to smile up at him, leaving his question unanswered. "Well, I'm here now, and it's so good to see you."

"Same." He held her by the shoulders and

looked her up and down. "Last time I saw you, you were still slogging away as a resident. You'd just gotten married." She did her best to hide the fact he'd basically sucker punched her in the feels, but obviously not well, because he hugged her once more. "I'm so sorry. Your father told me about Ben. What a horrible thing he did."

Horrible *doesn't begin to cover it.*

Inhaling deep, Morgan nodded, then stepped back again, forcing a tremulous smile. "Yes. Thanks. It was pretty bad."

The loss. The cheating.

She cleared her too-tight throat, then tucked her hair behind her ear, desperate to change the subject. "But I'm here and ready to work. Where's your partner?"

"Dr. Malik called just before you arrived and said he's on his way."

"Great." Morgan glanced down and noticed a tiny spot of mud on her wrist. *Crap.* She brushed it away fast, remembering the feel of Ely's thumb on her skin, and damn if her traitorous skin didn't tingle again. Annoyed with herself, she shoved all those messy emotions aside. "Um, if you don't mind, I'll pop into the restroom and freshen up."

"Absolutely. Take your time."

Alone, Morgan stared at her reflection in

the mirror. The new haircut, the new clothes, the same old wariness lurking in her eyes. *Get a grip, girl.* Once upon a time, she'd been a trusting fool. No more.

She washed her hands then headed out to the waiting room again.

"Perfect timing. Dr. Malik's here and waiting for us in the conference room," Dr. Greg said. "Since we're running a bit late already, maybe he can show you around the place in the morning. Don't want to be late for our dinner reservations in town. Afterward, Peggy and I will take you to the cottage where you'll be staying while you're here. Sound good?"

"Absolutely."

"Follow me, then." Dr. Greg led her down a hall lined with exam rooms that ended in a large, circular nurses' station from which other hallways spoked off, like a wheel. The conference room sat at the back of the facility, lined on one side with floor-to-ceiling tinted windows, giving them gorgeous views of the sunset and Puget Sound in the distance. You could still smell the fresh paint and drywall in the air. Morgan proceeded Dr. Greg in, then turned to greet the man sitting at the far end of the long table, overhead lights gleaming off his freshly showered damp hair, his brown skin glowing against his crisp white shirt.

Oh, no. No, no, no.

For a moment Morgan stood speechless. This could not be happening. Ely could not be the doctor she'd work with for the next month. Nope. Ten years with no contact at all, and now she'd seen him twice in one day. This was bad. So bad. Morgan did not handle surprises well anymore, and this was the second whopper in one day. Her pulse jackhammered against her temples and beat in her gums.

"Dr. Salas." Ely stood and walked down the length of the table, his tawny gaze unreadable. To the side, she felt Dr. Greg's gaze boring into her as well, the back of her neck prickling. She barely heard Ely's words over the thump on her own heart. "I hope your trip here was pleasant. Sorry I was late. I had to assist a stranded motorist. Got their vehicle stuck in a ditch."

He was acting like he didn't know her, like the accident in the ditch didn't happen.

Right. Okay. It took a moment for her brain to catch up to the reality racing around her and for her to realize that she needed to act, to respond, to do the job she'd come here for, because there was no alternative. She'd already given notice at her job in Boston and sublet her apartment there. Whidbey Island was her last resort—for the next month, at least. If this didn't work out, she'd have to find something else fast. She didn't have enough savings to survive long without a job. Six months in Africa had eaten through her nest egg.

Ely sat as well, across from her, still pretending he didn't know her from Adam. Maybe he didn't—not anymore. "This shouldn't take too long, Dr. Salas. Dr. Greg assures me you're the right person to fill the temporary vacancy, and at this late stage, I must believe him. He couldn't say enough good things about you."

She blinked at him, nodded, still trying to gather her thoughts, feeling oddly numb now.

"We're lucky to get her, Ely," Dr. Greg said. "Morgan's very in demand."

She wasn't, but appreciated the boost of confidence.

"Well, then." Ely steepled his fingers, watching her over the top of them. "Tell me why you chose our little island."

Our little island...

His gaze had gone chillier now, and she got the distinct impression he knew. He remembered their night together as well as she did. But he was pretending he didn't. Which meant he was lying. Morgan didn't deal well with liars, either. Not after Ben. Voice tight, she said, "I recently returned from a mission in Africa, and I want to do good and be part of a community."

"I see." He glanced down at her hands, clenched atop the table, then met her eyes again. "Dr. Salas, I won't lie."

Really? Her mind spun. *Because you just did, about us.*

"I have my concerns. Mainly the fact you don't have much GP experience. It says on your CV you worked as an ER physician in Boston. Is that correct?"

She nodded, nausea building inside her.

"And you're recently back from a mission trip in Africa as well. This clinic might be a big change for you. Perhaps too big. All that adrenaline-fueled medicine is a big contrast from Whidbey Island." He sighed, his gaze flicking to Dr. Greg as he flashed a rueful smile. "We do have our moments, though, right?"

Dr. Greg chuckled. "Right."

"This is what I want," Morgan said, struggling to salvage what was left of the situation. "Peace. Quiet. A chance to slow down and decide what to do next." She glanced out the windows, wishing she were out on the water. She always felt better on the water. "I like being by the sea."

The water had brought her here all those years ago, too.

"I've talked to her, Ely," Dr. Greg added. "She knows what to expect."

Do I?

Morgan was starting to doubt it now.

"I've still got my sailboat, too, Morgan," Dr. Greg chimed in, cutting through the roar of emotional clutter in her head. "Feel free to take *The Nightingale* while you're here. Please. I don't get out on her as much these days, with my hip replacement and all, but Ely takes good care of her for me. I'm sure he'd be delighted to take you out on the sound sometime."

Ely returned his colleague's smile, and Morgan's heart stuttered. His tawny eyes creased at the corners, and his dimples showed.

Stop! Abort! Abort!

She shook her head, straightening her spin.

Get it together. Now. Don't mess up this job. You need it.

The next hour passed swiftly. Her credentials were impeccable, as was her professional experience. She'd spent some time in family practice during her medical school rotations and had certainly seen her share of basic cases through the ER in Boston as well, so the adjustment shouldn't be as glaring as Ely thought. And Morgan expected this new practice would pose its own set of challenges, too.

"We're the best-equipped clinic on the southern half of the island and serve several communities, including Langley, Freeland, Clinton and Greenbank, as well as the small villages in between," Dr. Greg said once Ely's questions for her had run out. She answered them all as appropriately as possible, or at least she hoped she did, though she couldn't quite remember what she'd said.

Luckily, Dr. Greg kept talking, giving her something else to focus on besides Ely. "We can handle most things here. Ely's a double fellow in both general practice and pediatrics. He's also got extensive experience in ob-gyn. Our on-call schedule is pretty straightforward, too," Dr. Greg went on. "You'll have every second night and weekend on and the others off. Sound workable?"

She nodded. "Yep. I like to stay busy."

Busy had kept her sane the past two years.

"We're all sorted, then." Dr. Greg stood. "Morgan, let's go get some dinner, shall we? Ely, are you sure you won't join us? I can add another name to our reservation."

"No, thanks. Need to get home. But give my love to Peggy and have a wonderful trip.

Don't worry about anything here. We'll be fine." Ely pushed to his feet. "I'll check in on you tomorrow, Dr. Salas. Make sure you have everything you need."

"Okay," she said, but he was already gone. She watched his retreating back down the hallway. "I don't think he's okay with me being here."

"Ely's a tough nut to crack," Dr. Greg admitted, then shrugged. "He'll open up more as he gets to know you. You'll see."

Morgan's heart sank. Maybe Ely had it right, keeping their distance and pretending there was nothing between them. Working together every day would be hard enough. Maybe she should just keep her head down and get through it. More drama in life was not on her list of things she needed, and this job was supposed to be a fresh start, not a new source of complications—especially ones like Ely.

Dr. Greg put an arm around her shoulders and added, "Don't worry, Morgan." He walked her back out to the lobby, then turned off the lights. "Ely's a good man. You can trust him."

But that was the trouble. She didn't trust anyone anymore. Not after Ben. She'd been there, done that, had her heart and future trampled on to prove it. And no matter what she and Ely might have shared in the past, Morgan wasn't sure she could ever trust him—or another man—again.

Ely drove home to Wingate, the twin beams of his headlights glowing on the quiet two-lane road. His thoughts were anything but quiet, though, looping around again and again to Morgan. Seeing her in that ditch had been jarring enough. Then learning they'd be working closely together for the next month...

Well, he wasn't quite sure how that would turn out, but his instincts told him it wasn't good.

He liked his small circle of family and friends and didn't let new people in often. The sudden loss of his parents had taught him that letting people too close only led to pain and heartache.

So having her reappear in his life out of the blue was unsettling, to say the least. Then there was the old awareness, the connection, flaring bright and vibrant as ever between them. She'd tried to play it off, tried to pretend it wasn't there, but it was undeniable. Always had been. Sizzling between them whenever they were close. He'd never had that with anyone else. Not even Raina.

But it spooked him, too. Ely got through life these days by staying in control. Protecting those he cared for and making wise, logical decisions. By not taking risks.

And Morgan all but had a neon sign above her head flashing Risky As Hell.

Dammit. It was his own fault, really. No one else to blame. He should've insisted on reviewing the details of the person Dr. Greg had insisted was the best choice for his temporary replacement. But he'd been so busy schedulewise lately, between the clinic and Dylan starting a new year at school, that he'd gone with whatever Dr. Greg wanted. The man had become something of a surrogate father to Ely, and if the new person was good enough for Dr. Greg, they were good enough for Ely.

He just wished it wasn't Morgan.

Not because he didn't want to remember their night together, but because he still couldn't forget it.

Distracted, Ely turned onto the long drive up to the estate and sighed. He supposed he might not have connected the dots anyway, even if he had reviewed her files. On that long-ago night, he and Morgan had known each other only by first names. It had been all about feelings, not details.

He frowned and typed in the security code at the gate.

After their night together, he'd always pictured Morgan as a warm, inviting, friendly person. But today she'd seemed cold, distant, withdrawn toward him. What could've happened to cause such changes in her? And why would she not have told him who she was earlier that day in the ditch? It all made him even more curious about her and the person she'd become after all these years…

No. Stop it.

He couldn't afford to get curious about Morgan. Becoming entangled in her life beyond the professional would take more than he had to give, no matter how intriguing he might find her.

Ely parked in front of the house again, then stood a moment, breathing in the scent of fresh, growing things. Part of the land here had been turned into something of a nature preserve, helping the native plants and wildlife of the island to flourish, and being in nature always calmed him. Tonight, though, he kept returning to the look on Morgan's face during that meeting. The lines of stress at the corners of her mouth. The vulnerability in her gaze. The tremble in her jaw. The tip of his thumb tingled in remembrance of the velvety warmth of her skin on his earlier...

Enough.

Determined to put her out of his mind, he headed inside. With Dr. Greg leaving tomorrow, there was nothing he could do. They'd have to find a way to work it out and keep the clinic running until his partner returned from Australia. He'd keep his errant emotions in check. Forget how his pulse kicked up a notch whenever she was around. This was business. Nothing more.

Nope.

Nothing at all.

CHAPTER THREE

MORGAN AWOKE THE next morning and blinked up at the sun-streaked ceiling, taking a few seconds to realize she was at the cottage. After Dr. Greg and Peggy had dropped her off the previous night, she'd been so exhausted she'd gone straight to bed without noticing much. Now, water lapped against distant shores, and seagull cries pierced the air. Not an unpleasant way to wake up at all.

After a yawn and a stretch, she got up and brushed her teeth, then turned on the shower to let the water heat. The amenities here at the cottage were nothing fancy, but what the place lacked in sophistication, it made up for in charm. Lots of exposed beams and cozy furniture. Wood floors and old pictures from the area on the walls.

But as she stepped under the steamy spray, thoughts of her temporary new home dissolved into memories of Ely. She'd been so sure he'd recognized her, especially at the interview, yet he'd said nothing.

Morgan sighed. Maybe she should leave well enough alone. After all, she'd built the Ely from all those years ago in her mind into a near-perfect fantasy, and there was no way reality could live up to that. Honestly, she barely knew him. What if he was horrible?

Except Ely didn't seem horrible. Not really. Distant? Yes. But not horrible. Not like Ben, who she'd only discovered had been cheating on her after the car accident that had killed him—and left his mistress untouched in the passenger seat.

A cold chill ran down her spine, and she stuck her head under the warm spray to chase it away, along with her lingering hurt and shame.

Why didn't I see it? The signs of his betrayal.

God. She felt like such an idiot.

She rinsed the conditioner from her hair, then turned off the shower before drying off. At least she had today to get situated and acclimate herself to her new home before starting at the clinic.

Once she'd gotten ready and dressed in jeans and a comfy sweatshirt, Morgan finished unpacking. The cottage consisted of one bedroom, one bathroom, a nice-size open kitchen area complete with a mini washer and dryer combo, and a small living room with a fireplace. Kindling had been set in the fireplace, which was a nice touch, but Morgan had no idea how to light it and didn't want to risk burning down the place, so maybe she'd leave that for a chilly night in the future.

A set of double doors off the living room led to a nice back patio area, surrounded by woods leading down to the water beyond. Sunlight filtered through the towering evergreens, and for the first time since the ditch yesterday, her sense of optimism returned. Perhaps she had made a wise decision in coming here after all, even with Ely complicating things.

She could handle him. She'd handled worse.

Morgan checked the pantry and found the shelves fully stocked. She started a pot of coffee, then made herself breakfast. After eating, she pulled her long, dark hair back into a ponytail, slicked on some lip balm, put on hiking boots and set out to explore. Whidbey Island was known for its trails, and she followed a well-worn footpath through the woods, not stopping until she reached the edge of the tree line and her breath caught. A green meadow stretched in front of her, bordered on one side by the bay and on the other by the road. More sheep grazed nearby. A few of them looked up at her, but they were otherwise more interested in the grass. She walked on a bit longer, then returned to the cabin, surprised to find a tall blond man waiting for her there.

"Hello," he said as Morgan approached, extending his hand with a friendly smile. "You must be Dr. Salas. My name's Jeremy Nelson. I'm the chef at Wingate."

Wingate. Why did that name sound familiar? Oh, right. She'd read there was some huge estate here on the island, owned by a wealthy tech family. She shook his hand. "Nice to meet you."

"Sorry to intrude on your day off, but Ely's tied up with another patient, and he asked me to call you. My daughter isn't feeling well, and since we're practically neighbors, I drove over to see if you're free to see her."

"Sure." Morgan headed for the front door. "Let me just get my medical bag. Please, come in."

Jeremy followed her inside the cottage.

"Wow. I haven't been to the cottage in years," he said from the living room as Morgan went into the bedroom to grab her things.

"I'd forgotten how tiny it was. The landscaper for Wingate used to live here."

"Really?" Morgan changed out of her hiking boots into flats, grabbed her medical kit, then returned to his side. "Well, it's lovely. Perfect size for me. Shall we go?"

The drive only took a few minutes. As they went, Jeremy chatted about the places she should try to visit while she was there—Coupeville, Deception Pass, Ebey's Landing. Morgan nodded and smiled, but given her schedule, she'd have little free time. Maybe she'd come back for another visit. Or not, depending on how things went with Ely. Then they entered through a set of metal gates and drove up a long private drive to an estate that looked right out of the pages of *Architectural Digest*. All sparkling glass and cool steel reflecting the native flora and fauna. To the left of the large home was a large greenhouse area. To the right, a solar panel farm to harvest energy. Jeremy pulled to a stop under a side portico, and they got out. If the interior of the home was anywhere near as spectacular as the outside, Morgan was in for a treat.

Jeremy must've noticed her awed expression, because he chuckled. "The house is sixty-six thousand square feet total, with seven bedrooms, six kitchens and twelve bathrooms."

He opened the front door and led Morgan into a stunning foyer with gleaming parquet floors and wide-open space beneath soaring cathedral ceilings. A grand staircase curved gracefully up one side of the space to a balcony above, and an enormous abstract art–inspired chandelier sparkled in the sunlight streaming from skylights at least forty feet above them. The most striking features, though, were the floor-to-ceiling windows lining the entire opposite side of the house. They overlooked an immaculate deck and yard, a carpet of emerald-green grass stretching clear down to Mutiny Bay beyond. Her whole apartment back in Boston would've fit in that room.

"Wow. This place is spectacular," Morgan said, taking it all in. Over a massive stone fireplace hung a large portrait of a couple who seemed vaguely familiar. Something about the eyes…

"My daughter's upstairs," Jeremy said. "Gina's been complaining about her stomach hurting this morning. She vomited a few times, too. I gave her over-the-counter meds, but they haven't helped. I'm probably just overreacting, but…"

"No, it's fine. I'm happy to examine her. Better safe than sorry, I say." Morgan followed him up to the second floor. This space felt cozier, more lived in, though still light and airy. Jeremy took her to a pleasantly furnished bedroom in the corner. Elephants danced across a pink quilt atop a large poster bed. Beneath the covers was pale little girl who looked about seven. She had Jeremy's blond hair and wide brown eyes.

Morgan smiled and crouched beside the bed, pointing at a pink stuffed rabbit clutched in the little girl's hands. "Does your bunny have a name? I had a blue one named George when I was your age."

Gina eyed Morgan warily from between the rabbit's ears. "My tummy hurts. And I threw up. A lot."

"I'm sorry. Let's see what we can do about that, okay?" She straightened and pulled her stethoscope from her medical bag. "Can you lie flat so I can feel your tummy?"

The girl's gaze darted from Morgan to her father.

"Go on, honey," Jeremy said. "It's fine."

The child scooted down and put her arms by her sides, rabbit still held tight.

Upon palpation, Morgan didn't find any abdominal tenderness, which was good. Next, she checked Gina's throat for inflammation, but found nothing there, either. Pulse and temperature were good, too, as were her lungs.

"Well, I think you'll be just fine." Morgan finished her exam. "Nothing to worry about. But I am going to ask your dad to keep you in bed for the rest of the day and maybe tomorrow, too, just in case. Nothing to eat, but small sips of water when you get thirsty. I'll stop by tomorrow to see how you are."

She turned toward Jeremy and signaled for him to step out into the hall with her.

"I'm guessing it's just a stomach bug," she told him. "I'll give you my cell number, though, and please don't hesitate to call if there's any change in your daughter's condition. I suspect in a day or two, she'll be back to normal. Just keep her in bed today and let her sleep."

"Thank you." Jeremy gave a relieved sigh. "I know it's silly to worry, but she's all I've got. Do you have time for a coffee?"

Morgan checked her smart watch out of habit, but she had nowhere she had to be. "Okay."

"Good. Let me just tuck Gina in first."

Morgan waited for him, then followed Jeremy back downstairs.

"Are you sure? You don't need to go to any trouble for me," Morgan said. "I'm sure you're busy."

"No trouble at all. I've actually been up most of the night with Gina, so I could use the caffeine." He yawned, then smiled. "Honestly, you'd be doing me a favor. Talking to you will keep me from falling asleep."

She laughed as they walked into a large chef's kitchen at the back of the house, and Jeremy started a fresh pot of coffee. Morgan took a seat at a huge granite-topped island in the center of the room. Black-and-white tiles gleamed underfoot, and the appliances were all top-of-the-line stainless steel, including an Aga stove complete with double oven. Morgan looked out the wide windows over the farm-style sink while they waited for the brew to be done.

"Must be a dream to work in this kitchen," she said.

"It doesn't suck." Jeremy grinned and grabbed two white mugs from the tall cabinets surrounding the sink. Once the coffee maker beeped, he filled the mugs then carried them to the island, along with cream and sugar on a tray, before taking a seat on the stool beside Morgan's. "Seriously, though. Gina and I both love it here. Ely's parents built this house years ago, and it's one of a kind. Now that they're gone, it's fallen on Ely and his brother, Sam, to maintain it, though. Upkeep on a place like this isn't cheap or easy, but it's a labor of love for them, I think." He stirred sugar into his coffee. "Right now there's not much staff. Just me and the house-keeper most days. Have you met Mrs. MacIn-tosh yet? She looks after your cottage, too."

"Oh. No, I haven't." Her brain had glitched there a second, over the fact Ely owned this magnificent place. "What did Ely's parents do, exactly? This place must've cost a for-tune to build."

"It did." Jeremy narrowed his gaze. "Ely's father started Malik Electronics. I'm sure you've heard of it."

Of course she had. Anyone living on the planet had heard of the tech giant, especially after it had recently merged with another company that produced half of the world's laptops. Her mouth dried, and she gulped more coffee to cover it. She should have con-nected the dots last night at the clinic, but then she'd been otherwise occupied trying not to have a breakdown after Ely's big re-veal. *Wow.* Now the familiarity of the people in that portrait over the fireplace made sense. He had his father's eyes. And they were rich.

Like *Forbes 100* wealthy. Which meant that Ely was officially a billionaire.

One more surprise to add to the list. She should probably be used to them by now. She wasn't.

While she was still trying to stop her foot from tapping against the rung of her stool, Jeremy fixed a plate of what looked like freshly baked cookies, then returned to the island. "Here," he said, winking as he held them out to her. "You look like you could use one of these."

Trembling, she took a cookie—chocolate chip, still warm from the oven—and bit into it without looking. It was delicious, not that she noticed much. "Sorry. I just… I had no idea about Ely. About…" She gestured toward the kitchen as a whole, her half-eaten cookie still in hand. "All this."

Jeremy winced. "Please don't tell him I said anything. He's kind of sensitive about it, which is understandable. And really, he's just like everybody. You wouldn't know about his family or his fortune by talking to him. Or Sam."

"I'm sorry." She swallowed hard. "Who's Sam?"

"Ely's younger brother." His expression went a bit dreamy, and Morgan suspected there was something more there, but she didn't feel comfortable asking. "They're both very down-to-earth. In fact, last year they started opening Wingate for tours three days a week. The donations go toward helping local farmers during tough times. Plus, Ely also rents out some of the other buildings for receptions and stuff. And there's also the Halloween costume ball to raise funds for all the local shelters—animal and human. I stay pretty busy because of it all." Jeremy glanced toward the door. "Sounds like Ely coming."

Sure enough, the man they'd been discussing walked in, freezing as he saw Morgan. "Uh, hello. What are you doing here?"

"She came to check on Gina," Jeremy said. "I'll get you some tea, Ely. Just a splash of milk."

Ely nodded, then focused on Morgan again, his expression wary. "Everything all right?"

"Fine," Morgan said, hoping it sounded more confident than she felt. Not about her abilities. Morgan was an excellent physician, and she knew it. But her personal life was another matter. "Gina has a stomach bug. I ordered bed rest today, then she should be recovered tomorrow."

"She's napping now," Jeremy added, returning with Ely's tea. "Mrs. MacIntosh is keeping an eye on her while I came down to tend to these cookies."

"Thanks." He took a sip, then asked Jeremy, "Where's Dylan?"

"Out back, with the gardener. As usual."

Dylan? Morgan was having trouble keeping up with all these new names.

Jeremy sighed. "Well, I should get back upstairs to my daughter. Unless there's anything else you need from me, Ely? Thank you again, Dr. Salas, for stopping by. I'll let you know if anything changes tonight with Gina's condition."

Ely waited until his chef left, then turned to Morgan. "Let me show you the backyard area."

It wasn't a question, so she couldn't really refuse. She tried anyway, needing time and space to process all that she'd learned. Not to mention the fact she wasn't ready to be alone with Ely again. Not with her pulse racing and adrenaline coursing through her system whenever he was near. She slid off her stool onto less-than-steady legs. "Um, maybe another time, actually." She started slowly inching toward the hallway behind her. "Your estate is lovely, by the way." Her nerves were firing on all cylinders now, for some reason, and if she wasn't careful, things would become awkward. Or more awkward than they already were, anyway.

"Morgan," he said, the look in his eyes leaving her no doubt that he remembered her now. "We need to talk."

Oh, God.

Well, if she'd learned anything from the last few months of her marriage to Ben it was that communication, even when painful, was necessary. Letting things go unsaid or fester was not good.

So, left with little choice, Morgan followed him out the back door of the kitchen and onto a large flagstone patio. The sea-scented air surrounded them, and the sun finally broke through the clouds above, heating her already warm face. They followed a gravel path away from the house and down a gently sloping hill toward the water. Morgan kept pace with Ely's longer strides as a taut silence fell between them.

"I'm assuming you know about my family," Ely said once they'd stopped near the rocky shoreline. "And you probably have questions."

About so many things.

But she never got the chance to ask, because Ely rushed on.

"The money doesn't matter to me, in case you wondered. And as far as the locals are concerned, I'm just Dr. Malik, or Ely. All this other stuff—" he gestured toward the house and grounds "—I keep because it's a tribute to my parents. Their legacy. Not mine. Someday it will all be donated to the island. I just want to help people and do what I love, in a place that's important to me."

"Okay." Her paltry response was all she could manage. The fact he hadn't just come right out and told her triggered her worst fears, despite his intentions. Granted, he had a right to his privacy, too, but after their shared past, she wished he'd just been honest with her up front. But it seemed there were a lot of things she'd wished for with Ely that never came true. Just like Ben.

Ely turned to her again, his tawny gaze intense. "I've wondered about you over the years. If you'd gone on to accomplish all those dreams you'd had. You've become a doctor. Good for you. Not that I ever doubted it. You were always so determined. Nothing would've stood in your way, Morgan."

It wasn't true. Too many of her dreams had fallen by the wayside or been lost.

Too many hopes had been crushed.

Morgan stared out at the water, swallowing hard against the constriction in her throat, old hurts and grief squeezing her chest. "I guess we both got what we wanted."

He scowled, kicking a pebble with the toe of his boot. "Maybe."

Why didn't you ever contact me? Didn't I mean anything to you?

She wanted to yell, scream, something, but stuffed it all down instead. The reality was people's actions spoke way louder than their words. Another lesson she'd learned the hard way from Ben. If Ely had wanted to find her during the last ten years, he would have. The fact he hadn't was surely answer enough.

Ely knew he'd hurt her all those years ago, but life had not gone as planned for him, either. He'd been home a week when he'd gotten the call from Raina that she was pregnant. They'd dated off and on at college before finally breaking it off before Ely had ever met Morgan. They'd been careful when they'd slept together, but obviously not careful enough. When he'd found out, his world had shifted. Family was the most important thing to Ely, and he was determined to make sure his son never had a day when he didn't know how much Ely loved him. He'd made his choices then and there, and they didn't involve Morgan.

But now, things were different. For both of them. Life had changed him from the carefree boy he'd been back then. Changed her, too, apparently. In ways he was only just discovering. Seeing her again, being around her, had his emotions in turmoil. His heart pounded, and his blood sang in his veins. Mouth dry, he started to say something, then stopped himself. Maybe it was too soon. Or too late.

Tell her. Tell her the truth.

"I was going to call you," Ely blurted out, his voice rough as he watched the choppy water of the bay, feeling about as bleak and beaten as the craggy gray rocks along the shoreline. "But things happened, Morgan. Things I'd never expected." Then he paused, took a deep breath. "Are you happy?"

Morgan shivered, wrapping her arms tighter around her middle, like a shield. "I haven't been for a while, but I'm getting there." She sighed and stared down at her toes. "I've been through a lot the past two years."

"I'm sorry," he said, for lack of anything better. The ache in her tone tugged inside him.

She nodded. "Me, too."

They stood there a moment, neither saying

anything, the air between them thick with possibilities and penitence.

Finally, she sighed and turned back toward the house. "I should go. Thank you for the tour."

He followed Morgan up the hill, not looking at the sway of her hips in the jeans she wore. Nope. Only to have her catch her foot on a rut and stumble back into him. Ely caught her elbow, the flowery smell of her shampoo surrounding him as her hair brushed his chin. The thump of blood in his gums grew stronger. He held on a second longer than necessary before stepping back and letting her go, fingertips tingling. Touching her felt good. Too good.

"Okay?" he asked, the word emerging rougher than he'd intended.

"Fine," Morgan mumbled, her cheeks pink and her gaze darting anywhere but at him. "Sorry."

Then, without warning, she started crying. Not sobs, just silent tears trickling down her cheeks. He froze, no idea what to do. Was this his fault? Perhaps he never should've brought up the past.

Then, to make matters worse, he reached up and cupped her cheek, swiping away a tear with his thumb without thinking. His breath stuttered, and his gut cramped.

Halt! Back away slowly!

Instead, he moved closer, lowering his voice to a near whisper. "What is it? What's wrong? Did you hurt yourself? Is this my fault?"

She waved him off and moved back, scowling as she searched her pockets. "I'm fine. I just… I don't know what's wrong with me."

Ely pulled out the packet of tissues he always kept close for his son in case of emergencies and handed them to her, chewing his lower lip. "Well, and if it helps at all, I swear I didn't know it was going to be you filling in for Dr. Greg. He'd given me your files and all ahead of time, but I didn't have a chance to read them. I trusted his judgment." He hesitated, then added, "I still do."

The weight in his chest lightened when he realized it was true. He and Morgan might have issues, but he did not doubt her medical abilities. Not at all.

"I'm not crying about that," she muttered, then turned away. "Or not only that. I don't know."

He hated seeing her upset like this and disliked even more thinking he might be the cause of it. "I'm sorry anyway."

"Stop saying you're sorry." She frowned. "It doesn't help anything. Show me instead."

Oh, boy. Oops.

Seemed he'd stepped in it again somehow. He swallowed another apology.

A beat passed, then two. Morgan finally met his gaze again. "I was married. My husband cheated on me. Now he's dead."

Did you kill him?

The words hovered on the tip of his tongue before he squashed them. This was no time to be flippant. And he was sure there was way more to that story that he was not privy to. Maybe in time she'd tell him. Until then, he needed to mind his business. He rubbed the back of his neck as she yanked another tissue from the plastic packet in her hand, still scowling.

"And don't look at me like that. I don't want your pity."

The last thing he felt for Morgan was pity. If anything, he admired her strength, her fortitude for surviving whatever she'd endured with this deceased husband of hers. While she dabbed at her cheeks, he turned slightly to give her some privacy, staring down the shoreline to the place where they'd first met all those years ago.

She'd been working with a sailing crew

going up the coast. Ely had been with his friends, having a cookout. By the time the introductions were made, the sky had become a riot of pinks and purples and golds. He could still picture Morgan, standing near the flames of their roaring bonfire, her bright smile rivaling the full moon above. Petite and curvy, with long brown hair and big blue eyes, her laugh had burned like a wildfire through his veins, and he'd been a goner. Couldn't help himself. Made excuses to his friends and led her away to where they'd had some privacy.

They'd talked a bit, between kisses. She'd been in her last year of premed, and he'd been ready to start his first residency. They'd agreed no last names, wanting to keep the magic of the moment alive. Then, as a lullaby of music and merriment drifted from the beach beyond, they'd made love. He'd been her first. She'd been the last woman he'd allowed himself to be so open with.

Afterward, they'd lain beneath the stars, the night breeze gentle on their skin, holding each other. She'd told him about her dreams, how hard she'd worked, holding two jobs to make ends meet and make up for what her scholarships didn't cover. He'd held her and listened, not saying much about himself. Not wanting her to see him differently because of who he was.

And the next morning, she'd left to sail back to San Diego.

"I wish you didn't have to go."

"Me, too. I gave you my cell number. You'll come visit me at Northwestern?"

"I will."

But he never had. Never called. Never visited. Had never seen her again.

Until now.

Heaviness weighed down his chest as he turned to face Morgan again now. His logical brain said to leave well enough alone, forget the past and just get through the next month. But the other part of him, the part sore with nostalgia and regret, forced him to say, "I'm here, if you want to talk."

"Talk?" She gave a derisive snort. "I'm tired of talking about the late Ben Morton. He cheated on me. And I didn't find out until the car accident that killed him because his mistress was with him that day. Sitting in the passenger seat. She walked away without a scratch." She blinked away more tears, her cheeks flushed, and his gut cramped.

"It was on the news, Ely. Everyone at the hospital. All our friends, family. They all knew. I tried to keep going as normal, but that's part of the reason I eventually went to Africa. Just to get away from it for a while. That's why I wanted to come here, too. Because no one would know me or my past. It could be a fresh start. And then you…you…"

Damn. He'd screwed it all up for her.

Now he felt bad. Really bad. He hadn't known and there wasn't much he could do about it now, but still.

"Come on," he said at last, continuing up the hill toward the house, feeling like a ton of bricks sat on his shoulders. "Best get inside. Those clouds on the horizon look like rain."

They returned to Wingate in silence, Ely sneaking glances at Morgan to make sure she was okay. They'd just reached the patio again when a high-pitched voice rang out from the side of the house, followed by a small dark-haired boy with a football barreling straight at him.

Suddenly, those bricks disappeared, and he felt a thousand pounds lighter again. Ely swooped his son into his arms and twirled him around, laughter filling the air.

"Daddy! Play football with me before lunch. Please?" Then Dylan's gaze locked on Morgan. "Who's that?"

CHAPTER FOUR

CONSIDERING WHAT SHE'D been through already on the island, Morgan's surprise threshold had long blown past its limit. She paused midsniffle and did a double take between Ely and the boy in his arms. Same dark hair, same features, but the eyes were different. Where Ely's eyes were a light golden-brown, the boy's gaze was sea foam green. So. Ely had a child. Huh.

"Uh." Ely set his son down, then cleared his throat, shuffling his feet. "Morgan, I'd like you to meet my son, Dylan. Dylan, this is Dr. Morgan Salas."

The little boy peered up at her, his football now tucked under one arm. "Nice to meet you."

"Nice to meet you, too." The kid was supercute, and she found herself smiling despite her rapidly drying tears. Morgan loved kids. Which made the fact she couldn't have any of her own now even more tragic. She crouched in front of the boy, smiling. "How old are you, Dylan?"

"I'll be ten in December," he said, looking enormously proud of himself.

As she made the mental calculations in her head, her smile faltered. Dylan would've been born shortly after she and Ely had been together, so…

Guess that explained why he'd never called.

Bile burned hot in her throat. No. Just no. Not another cheater.

Ely inhaled deep and raised his chin, as if steeling himself for battle. "Dylan, go toss your ball around while Dr. Salas and I talk. I'll be there in a minute."

She waited until the boy was out of hearing range before asking, "Ten years old? Seriously, Ely?"

He shook his head and looked away. "It's not what you think."

Another red flag went up in her brain. Ben used to tell her that, too.

Bastard.

"Daddy, I'm hungry." Dylan suddenly ran up to them again. "Can I have a snack?"

"Go check with Jeremy," Ely said, ruffling his son's hair.

"What about Dr. Salas?" Dylan peered up

at Morgan. "Can you stay for a snack, too? I'll show you my room. You can see my model boats. I love boats. Do you sail? Daddy does. Maybe we can all go out sometime?"

Morgan glanced between Ely and his son, her cheeks tight and her body tense. "And I'd love to see your room sometime, but I can't stay now. I need to get back to my cottage. Maybe later?"

The little boy nodded then rushed off once more.

Leaving Morgan and Ely alone again.

"Right, well…" He looked painfully awkward. Good. That made two of them.

"Right." She shoved her hands in her pockets, feeling far too vulnerable and raw for her liking. Despite her barriers, Ely had a way of cutting her down to the bone. Even more reason to keep clear of him outside work. "Goodbye, Ely."

Ely winced. "Wait, Morgan. I—"

"Save it. Really. We're work colleagues, Ely. Nothing more. How you choose to conduct your life is your affair." Inside, though, she was seething. Her skin felt too tight, and heat clawed up her neck regardless of the cool breeze off the water. She hated being the last to know things. Being on the outside. Secrets. And while Ely hadn't outright lied to her, he hadn't been exactly forthright, either, so same difference.

Their gazes snagged, but then an impenetrable, businesslike facade shuttered his face, and it was like a door slamming between them.

"I'll see you tomorrow, then," he said, his tone icy.

He walked away, and Morgan followed the trail to her cottage, grumbling to herself all the way about stupid men and their stupid choices. Lost in thought, she barely registered the fact she'd reached the woods surrounding the cottage until a strange female voice called out, jarring her. Morgan stopped in her tracks and peered through the evergreens to see an older woman waving from the cottage's porch.

"Hello, Dr. Salas," the woman said as Morgan neared. "I'm Mrs. MacIntosh, the housekeeper at Wingate. Wanted to check in on you and make sure you were settled."

"Hi." Morgan shook her hand. "I'm sorry if you've been waiting long. I was just up at Wingate, checking on Jeremy's daughter. Do come inside. And please, call me Morgan."

They went into the cottage, and Morgan hung her jacket on a hook by the door, offering to take Ms. MacIntosh's, but the woman declined.

"Hope this place is working out for you okay," the older woman said while Morgan went to the kitchen to start a pot of coffee. "Heard you had quite a drive onto the island yesterday."

Yikes. Word traveled fast around here. Morgan winced. "Does everyone on the island know?"

"Probably. This end of it, anyway." Mrs. MacIntosh laughed. "But don't worry. People in the area are just interested in the new doc and how our Ely swooped in and saved you."

"Well, I don't know about saving." Morgan bristled. She was hardly a damsel in distress. Helpless female wasn't her preferred look. "I would've figured a way out on my own eventually."

She started the coffee maker, then walked back out into the living room to find Mrs. MacIntosh lingering by the door. "Please, sit down."

"Oh, I can't stay. I have to get back to work. I'm already late." The older woman grasped the doorknob and smiled. "Just wanted to introduce myself and let you know I'll pop by in the morning to clean the place. After that, my schedule is three days a week. That's what Dr. Greg arranged, if that works for you."

Morgan had never had a housekeeper before, but she didn't want to be rude, so she nodded. "Okay."

She spent the rest of the afternoon tinkering around, staying busy so she wouldn't dwell on her discussion earlier with Ely. Why did she have to be so aware of him as a man? She didn't want to fall in love again. Didn't want another relationship. Didn't want romance. Especially with a man who hadn't been completely honest with her. She'd been there, done that. Had the scars to prove it. No. She was safer, happier, on her own. And yes, working together at the clinic would make keeping her distance from Ely more difficult, but it was necessary.

One month. Thirty-one days.

Then she could get on with her life and leave Ely Malik behind for good.

CHAPTER FIVE

MORGAN CRANKED THE heat in her rental car as she drove to the clinic the next morning. Wind howled and rain hurled against the windows of the sedan, and she clicked the wipers higher. Perhaps she should've worn a rain poncho instead of the well-cut beige suit she'd chosen for her first official day at work, but she'd wanted to look nice. She had an umbrella, so it should be fine.

According to the schedule the clinic had emailed her last night, they'd see patients in the morning, then she'd accompany Ely on home visits that afternoon. In between, Morgan planned to stop by Wingate to check on Gina as well, although she was pretty sure Jeremy would've called if there'd been any problems.

She navigated the twisty two-lane roads, doing her best to focus on the day ahead and not the past, but damn if that conversation hadn't stirred something up inside her again. She'd even dreamed about Ben last night, which hadn't happened in a long time. Anger sizzled inside her, and she gripped the steering wheel tighter with both hands. Ben didn't deserve that prime real estate in her brain after what he'd done. Morgan shifted in her seat, a familiar painful pinch of shock in her chest making her antsy. Each time she thought of that day, that phone call from the state police, it was like she was right back there again—phone slipping from her damp hand, legs threatening to buckle, throat choking her. Even after two years, the visceral explosion inside her was still strong, like a wound that refused to heal.

It was the reason she worked so hard, stayed busy. Because then she didn't have time to think, time to feel. An old coping pattern of hers, one that had probably kept her marriage to Ben going far longer than it should have. In their final six months together, they'd barely been a couple, barely talked to each other more than passing pleasantries, barely had sex at all. She'd been too emotionally drained from losing her baby, and he hadn't known how to deal with her trauma because of that or his own. So, they'd fallen into a kind of weird half-life.

Not that any of that excused his infidelity. She'd not done that to him, and the fact he'd done that to her made her feel like a fool when the truth had finally come out after the accident. A stupid, trusting idiot.

Since then, she'd vowed never to be that vulnerable again. Never to feel that raw. Gone were her days of blindly accepting whatever someone told her as fact. No one got past her walls now without a fight.

Including Ely Malik.

She pulled into the clinic parking lot and pulled into one of the Staff Only spots, then cut the engine, steadfast in her resolve to keep things professional. Morgan exited her vehicle with her umbrella over her head, then ran for the front entrance. Some other staff were already there, including Ely. He was talking with two women at the front desk, looking far better than should be allowed in a dark gray suit and burgundy-striped tie. She cleared her throat and wrangled her umbrella closed in the vestibule before entering the lobby.

"Good morning, Dr. Salas," Ely greeted her from behind the large, circular reception desk. His crooked smile gave her heart an unwanted tug.

Stop it.

"Once you've put your things away, I'll

give you a tour before we start seeing patients."

"Thank you." Morgan dropped her purse off in Dr. Greg's office before returning to the desk. "Ready for duty."

He introduced her to the rest of staff. Sandy, an older LPN who handled scheduling surgeries and procedures as well as assisting patients in the office. Didi, the receptionist, who was in her midtwenties with a blue streak in her hair that matched her scrubs and a sparkly diamond nose stud. Joan, the radiology tech, and Mark, who ran the lab. Plus, there were several certified medical assistants who kept the back clinic running like clockwork.

They started down one of the halls, and Ely pointed out exam rooms, procedure rooms, ultrasound and X-ray facilities, the lab, and a small ambulatory surgery area. "We do our own minor surgeries here. More complicated cases need to be transferred to either Oak Harbor or Seattle General, depending on the severity. There's an air ambulance service, if needed. Even so, we're equipped to handle most emergencies in a pinch." He glanced over at her. "How are your surgery skills?"

"Good," Morgan said. "I handled a variety of things out in the field in Africa."

"Excellent." Ely looked impressed. "Well,

if you ever have questions or need a second opinion, call me. You have support options."

"Noted."

The morning went by faster than Morgan had expected. Her full roster included mainly colds and flus, rechecks, and the occasional laceration that needed stitching. After they finished seeing everyone, Ely ordered in lunch and the staff ate together in the break room to get to know each other.

"I heard you went up to Wingate to treat Gina," Didi said, sliding into the chair next to Morgan's at the long table. "Jeremy and I are good friends."

"Yep, I did," Morgan said, amazed at how quickly news spread on the island. "Jeremy's great. I'll tell him you said hello when I stop by later to check on his daughter."

"Hey, Doc?" Sandy said from the other end of the table, and both Ely and Morgan looked her way. The older nurse cringed. "Sorry. Dr. Malik. I got a call from Karen Greene right before clinic ended this morning. She's having some anxiety. Doesn't think her baby's moving as much. Can you stop by and see her this afternoon?"

"How many weeks is she now?" Ely asked.

"Thirty-six, barely. She's booked into Oak Harbor for delivery two weeks from now."

"You're inducing her?" Morgan frowned. "Is she high-risk?"

"No. Karen's thirty-three, and this is her first baby." Ely wiped his mouth with a napkin. "But her husband's a long-haul trucker and wants to be there for the birth, so we agreed to induce her while he's here. Given her clean medical history, I don't see any harm." He turned back to Sandy. "My schedule's pretty full this afternoon. Could you stop by first, Sandy, then call me with an update?"

"Sure thing."

"Great." He checked his watch, then glanced at Morgan. "As soon as you're finished, we can go."

On the way to their first home visit, Morgan didn't say much, just stared out the window beside her at the passing scenery. Which was fine with him, since he was still churning through their conversation behind his house yesterday and the implications of it. He couldn't blame her for her anger and resentment toward her deceased husband after hearing what the man had done, but it was still hard for him to reconcile the woman Morgan Salas was now to the fantasy version he'd carried in his head for years. Then again, he tended do that, he knew. Romanticize things from his past, turn them into something bigger and grander than they really were. He'd done that with his parents after their deaths, too. That had never happened with his marriage to Raina, though, probably because she was still around, reminding him of why they were not a good match, even though they remained cordial to coparent Dylan.

They rounded a bend in the road, and he hazarded a glance at her again, finding Morgan watching him now, and the hairs on his forearms stood on end with wariness. He was a man who valued his privacy, sometimes to his own detriment. He didn't like talking about himself, a by-product of growing up in a family where his parents' every move had been splashed all over the tabloids. He didn't want to live like that. Didn't want to put Dylan through that, either. So, he kept a low profile, both professionally and personally.

"Your son is very cute," she said after a moment, her gaze slightly narrowed. "How long have you been married?"

He gave her a side glance, uncomfortable heat prickling up from beneath the collar of his white button-down shirt. *Relax. She's just being polite. You can open up a little, especially after what she told you.* Except it was difficult. So difficult. He rolled his stiff shoulders and stared straight ahead. "I'm divorced."

"Oh. I'm sorry."

He could've just left it there, but he kept talking for some reason he didn't want to examine too closely. "Things with Raina, my ex-wife, didn't work for a lot of reasons. We were both too young, too driven in our own careers. Mainly, we were just too different. We tried to stay together for Dylan's sake, but it was better for everyone for us to part ways. We divorced two years ago."

Morgan nodded then stared out the window again, her expression unreadable. But he could imagine the wheels turning in her head as his old sense of failure burned hot and heavy in his gut. Ely wasn't a man who liked to fail. Even in a marriage that had been doomed from the start. Even with a woman he hadn't seen in ten years but had never forgotten. Their old connection still simmered just below his surface, and it terrified him. He didn't want to get involved with Morgan. Didn't want to get involved with anyone. Because that would mean risking his heart and his future, and he never wanted to do that again.

Luckily, before Morgan could ask him anything else, they arrived at their first patient's home, giving them work as a distraction. John Morris was an elderly man suffering from shortness of breath. He had a difficult time making it into the office, so house calls here were routine for Ely. Didn't stop the man's wife from apologizing continuously for putting them through a visit on such a rainy, miserable day.

"It's fine, Mrs. Morris," Ely reassured her. "We're happy to do it. This is Dr. Salas's first day, so it gives me a chance to show her where all the patients live. You're doing us a favor. No trouble at all."

"I've made you both a batch of brownies, just the same," Mrs. Morris said. "Let me get them while you two examine my John."

She went to the kitchen while Ely gave Morgan a rundown on the patient's condition.

"Mr. Morris is seventy-five and complains of shortness of breath for the last few days." Ely listened to the patient's lungs with his stethoscope, then stepped aside so Morgan could do the same.

"I'm fine." The patient harrumphed, flushed and drawn as he sat in his recliner in the living room. "Mildred's always worrying and fussing. I'm old, but I'm not dead yet."

Morgan caught Ely's eye and bit back a smile.

"Since we're here, why not let us check you over?" Ely asked. "Better safe than sorry, eh?"

He checked the patient's extremities for swelling, then took his temperature, which was elevated. "I'm guessing this is an upper respiratory infection," he said, straightening and hanging his stethoscope around his neck. "We'll treat you with antibiotics. Take it easy, John, and drink plenty of fluids. You should feel better again in no time."

"A little cold never killed anybody. And what about my animals?" The older man pointed out the window toward the animals grazing in the field. "Somebody's got to tend to the sheep."

"Mr. Morris, at your age a chest infection can become pneumonia if not treated properly," Morgan added. "Better a few days resting now than a week or more in the hospital later."

"Let me call your neighbor," Ely said, pulling out his phone. Small island practices offered services above and beyond the standard. "I'll see if Dave can keep an eye on your herd until you've recovered."

Mr. Morris scowled, looking like he wanted

to argue, but he was outnumbered and knew it. Finally, he scoffed and gave a dismissive wave, crossing his arms. "Fine. But make sure he can do it first."

While Ely made the call, Mrs. Morris returned with a huge plate full of brownies. She set them on the coffee table, then took a seat on the arm of her husband's chair. Ely got through to the neighbor, who was happy to help, then he returned to his patient.

"Dave's got you covered," he said, reaching for a brownie. They were the best on the island, even better than Jeremy's. Not that he'd tell his chef. He swallowed a delicious chocolaty bite, then smiled. "Amazing as always, Mildred."

"Glad you like them, Dr. Malik. I've packed a box of them for each of you to take with you."

Ely finished his brownie, then went over prescriptions and instructions with Mr. Morris. By the time they left, he noticed Morgan had downed not one but two brownies, and she groaned uncomfortably once they were back in his truck.

"Too full?" he asked, grinning as he started the engine. "I should've warned you not to overindulge at lunch. Same thing happened to me when I first started. I didn't want to be rude, so I ate everything my patients put in front of me. Now you'll know for next time." He signaled, then pulled back onto the main road. "As a rule, I visit our elderly, sick patients first to prevent minor ailments from becoming serious illnesses."

"Makes sense." Morgan fastened her seat belt. "And that was nice of you, making sure his sheep were handled." She smiled over at Ely, a genuine one this time, and his chest warmed. Man, he remembered that smile. More than he should. Sunny and bright and unguarded. He'd missed it.

So much for keeping things strictly professional.

Ely scowled and focused straight ahead again.

Enough of that.

Morgan continued talking, which he hadn't expected. "In the ER in Boston, we rarely saw the same patient twice. That's another reason I wanted a change. I'd rather get to know people. Figure out what makes them tick, what worries them. I believe that can help us treat them better."

"Agreed." He believed much the same, that medicine was more than tests and procedures. That to truly heal a person, you had to take a holistic approach—body, mind and spirit.

Ely drove on, tapping his thumb on the steering wheel. Huh. They agreed on something. Imagine that. After yesterday, he wasn't so sure he hadn't completely made up the synergy he'd felt with her that night on the beach. But nope. They did have things in common. Professionally, anyway. That was good for the clinic.

What about in the bedroom?

Uh…no. Where the hell had *that* come from?

He cleared his throat and shifted his weight, doing his best to eliminate the now-burgeoning swell of awareness inside him. Not going there. Not at all. His scalp tingled, and he resisted the urge to scratch it.

Concentrate on work. That's why you're here. The only reason you're here.

"On the downside, we get too attached to patients." He shrugged one shoulder to release some tension. "And when things go badly, it's harder because we know them so well." Over the years, Ely had lost several patients who'd been friends and mentors to him, and it never got easier. And wasn't that just the wet blanket he needed to calm down inside? Feeling more in control again, he straightened and leaned an elbow on the edge of the window beside him. "But this way of practicing medicine is worth it to me. It's what I like best about living here on the island. I've known most of these people my whole life."

Two more house calls followed—one to an elderly man with pulmonary edema and another to a child with chicken pox. Both cases were straightforward, and Morgan handled them well, her bedside manner easy and engaging. She seemed to really listen to each patient and put them at ease. Even Ely relaxed around her after a while.

"Who's next?" she asked once they'd climbed back into his truck again.

"Roger Cayman. He lives near Langley, the farthest distance from the clinic. Then there are two more who live closer, and we'll see them on the way back."

They passed Karen Greene's house on the way, and Ely got a bad feeling as he saw Sandy's car still parked out front. The nurse should've been done with a simple OB check by now. He signaled, then turned into the circular drive in front of the house to park. Checked his phone, but there was no signal.

Dammit.

"What's going on?" Morgan asked, her tone concerned.

"This is Karen Greene's house. The OB patient we discussed earlier in the break room.

Just want to pop in on Sandy and make sure everything's okay." He cut the engine and unbuckled his seat belt. "Be right back."

Sandy opened the front door before he got there, and he knew then there were issues. His LPN had been doing her job for years and had seen and done pretty much everything. It took a lot to rattle her, and based on Sandy's pale face and white-knuckled grip on the door frame, things were serious.

"I tried to call you," the nurse said. "But the service here is terrible."

"What's going on?" Ely asked, sidling around her to get into the house.

"Low fetal heart tones, around fifty. And Karen's water just broke. I can see the umbilical cord."

Damn. A probable cord prolapse.

Ely's pulse notched higher. If the umbilical cord became compressed too much during delivery, the baby would suffocate and die. Extremely bad news, especially on an isolated island, because if the baby did survive delivery, they'd need a NICU right away. Time was of the essence.

"What's happening?" Morgan rushed into the house beside him.

"Probable cord prolapse," he said, mind jumping ahead ten steps already. "We need to get Karen delivered ASAP. Have you done an emergency C-section?" Ely asked Morgan.

"Yes. Once in my OB rotation, and once in Africa." Her eyes widened. "Why?"

"The clinic is ten minutes away. Our surgery room is fully stocked. One of the GPs in Langley used to be an anesthesiologist. Sandy can call him now and he could meet us there."

From the back of the house, Karen screamed as another contraction wracked her body.

Decision made, Ely went into emergency mode, giving orders as he walked down the hall toward Karen's bedroom, medical bag in hand. "Sandy, get ahold of Dr. Lake. Tell him we need him at our clinic stat for anesthesia. Then, when you get a moment, reschedule the rest of our house calls this afternoon to another day. Morgan, call Seattle General and tell them to dispatch their air crew to our clinic. Then call Didi and tell her to have the CMAs prep the surgery room so it's ready to go when we get there. I'm going to insert a catheter to help relieve some of the pressure from her bladder off the umbilical cord and buy us some time to get her to the clinic."

It was a tense time, but the three of them managed to get the patient prepped and loaded into the back of Ely's truck, Sandy by Karen's side as they drove to the clinic. By the time they got there, thankfully Dr. Lake had arrived and the staff had everything in place. Ely and Morgan scrubbed up together while Sandy monitored the baby's heartbeat in the OR.

"Ely?" Morgan asked, rinsing off her hands and forearms.

"Yes?"

"How many C-sections have you done in the last two years?"

He took a deep breath and stepped off the pedal to shut off the water, keeping his hands and forearms elevated. "None. Why?"

"Let me take the lead on this, then," Morgan said firmly. "The baby will need your pediatric skills the moment it's delivered."

Ely backed into the surgery room ahead of Morgan and slid his arms into the sterile gown one of the medical assistants held for him. "But it was my decision to operate. If anything goes wrong, it should be my responsibility."

"For the record?" She slid into her own gown, then waited while an assistant put on her gloves and tied a mask on her face. "I agree with your decision. But if we want to save them both, the best chance that baby has is for you to stand by to resuscitate, if needed. Okay?"

Ely wasn't one to give up the fight, but it made sense. He gave a curt nod. "Let's do it."

The patient was on the table already with Dr. Lake ready to administer the anesthetic. Karen stared up at Ely, eyes wide and overly bright with fear. He squeezed her hand and spoke slowly, reassuringly. "We'll do everything we can, I promise. Once this is over, the air ambulance will take you and the baby to Seattle General. I'll fly with you to make sure you get settled properly, okay?"

"What about my husband?" Karen asked, tears welling. "He wants to be here."

He glanced at Sandy, who nodded. "He's on his way. Just relax. This will be over soon."

She nodded, gripping his hand even tighter. "Please save my baby."

"We're going to do our best," Morgan assured her.

Within seconds of Dr. Lake administering the anesthetic, Karen was out. Ely stood opposite Morgan as she began the procedure, making a deep, steady incision across the patient's abdomen, then another through the uterine wall and the placenta before reaching in and lifting out the baby and placing it in

Ely's waiting hands. A few clamps, a quick snip and the cord was cut.

"It's a girl," he informed the room. "Good size, too, considering she's early."

He moved over to a separate table set up for the infant. The baby was blue and unresponsive, and he quickly cleared the tiny baby's mouth and nose of mucus clogging her airway, then checked her pulse. Still slow. Precious seconds ticked by. No change.

"We need to intubate." Ely inserted a small breathing tube into the infant's trachea, then attached a bag to force air into the baby's lungs. Sandy placed a hand lightly on the infant's chest, her solemn expression slowly replaced by a smile. "Heartbeat's improving, and baby's pinking up nicely." A collective sigh of relief echoed through the OR. "She's going to make it."

Ely removed the breathing tube, and moments later the welcome sound of a newborn's cries filled the air. Morgan nodded, her blue eyes shining with triumph and appreciation over her mask, and Ely's chest warmed with gratitude and grace and something far closer to affection than he was ready for. She turned then to finish closing on the patient's surgery while he continued cleaning up the baby and getting the infant ready for transport.

It was another half hour before Morgan had finished with Karen, and Ely rolled and stretched his stiff shoulders and neck. Finally, he could breathe again. He and Morgan walked back into the scrub area together, peeling off their gloves and soiled gowns, tossing them in the biohazard bin before scrubbing up once again, a sense of satisfaction palpable between them.

"The patient did well," Morgan said, her voice quieter now, faint lines of fatigue at the corners of her eyes. Ely wondered how much that surgery had taken out of her. Having experience was one thing. Being called to perform at the drop of a hat was another. "Karen's beginning to come around already. Hopefully the air transport will be here soon. How's the baby?"

"Good. The sooner we get them both to Seattle General, though, the better I'll feel. The baby will need round-the-clock care in the NICU for the next few days, but I think the biggest danger is past." He sighed and grabbed paper towels from the dispenser on the wall. "You did fantastic in there, Morgan. Thank you."

"You're welcome." Her cheeks pinkened slightly, and he felt an unaccountable urge to hug her tight. Instead, Ely finished drying his hands far more aggressively than necessary before tossing his used towels away and making a beeline for the door.

Coward.

Maybe, but at least his heart was safe. He could not allow himself to care about Morgan again. Not that way. She'd be gone at the end of the month. He had to remain logical about this. Had to remain in control. Even if his pounding pulse and buzzing knees already said he was too late.

Morgan joined him and the rest of the staff in the hall after she'd finished cleaning up, thankfully not mentioning his hasty retreat.

Ely swallowed hard against the lump of unwanted yearning in his throat and instead focused on the people around him. "Nice job, everyone. Especially you, Dr. Salas. We—"

The loud whirr of approaching helicopter blades overhead cut his speech short. Which was just as well, he supposed, given the turmoil inside him. He had to get a handle on all these feelings she evoked in him without even trying—need, nostalgia, regret, want— if he had any hope of keeping things professional between them.

Head down, Ely helped Morgan wheel Karen's gurney out of the surgery room and down the hall to the back entrance. The helipad for the clinic was still under construction, so the air ambulance landed in an open field adjacent to them.

"My baby?" a groggy Karen asked as they loaded her into the helicopter.

"Got her right here," Sandy said, handing the infant in to her mother once Karen was settled by the paramedics.

A loud horn sounded from the parking lot, and a huge semi screeched to a stop. A burly man with a beard and baseball hat climbed out and hurried toward them. "Sweetheart, I got here as fast as I could." Karen's husband promptly started crying the moment he saw his daughter for the first time. "She's the most beautiful thing ever."

There was enough room for one more person, and Ely and Morgan exchanged a look.

"Go on, then," Morgan said after a moment. "You promised her in the OR you'd be there."

He grinned—couldn't help it. "I did." He shouted to be heard over the roar of the rotors. "I'll be back in a few hours to give you an update."

"Take your time," she called back, waving. "I'll hold the fort down here while you're gone."

CHAPTER SIX

MORGAN WROTE UP her notes on the surgery and stuck around to handle phone calls and anything else that might pop up until closing, then she left. It was well after five now, but she still wanted to stop by Wingate on her way back to the cottage to check on Gina.

Jeremy had followed her advice and kept the little girl in bed for the day, and now Gina was bouncing off the walls with energy. With the patient feeling better, the recheck was fast, and Morgan ended up in the kitchen again with Jeremy afterward, glad to have made a new friend. She told him about the emergency C-section while he made them tea.

"Sounds like you had an eventful first day," he said. "I saw a snippet about it on the local news. The air ambulance getting called in always makes for a big headline."

Morgan smiled. "I keep forgetting how quiet things are usually on this island. I hope emergencies aren't a regular occurrence around here. I had enough of that in Africa."

"They're not." Jeremy slid onto the stool beside hers and rested his elbow on the black granite countertop and his chin in his palm. "You look exhausted."

"I feel exhausted." She grinned. But more than fatigue, it was the growing ache inside her that bothered Morgan. The one that had been growing since she'd walked into Karen Greene's house earlier today. Which was silly, honestly. As a physician, she saw lots of pregnant patients. They'd never bothered her before, not even after her own disastrous outcome. But something about today... She sighed and rubbed her tired eyes. Seeing Karen come so close to losing her precious baby today had brought back the grief and guilt and shame about her own ectopic pregnancy. The knot of sadness in her chest tightened. That, as much as the surgery, zapped her energy reserves. But it was too early to share that with Jeremy. They'd just met. So, she fell back on her standard excuse. "I just need a good night's sleep."

Liar.

What she needed was a hug and a cuddle. From Ely.

Stop it.

"Do you know how Gina and I came to live here at Wingate?" he asked over the rim of his mug. The always cheerful Jeremy looked far more serious now than she'd ever seen him. "We moved in after my partner, Scott, died of a brain aneurysm. One second he was fine, the next he was gone." The edge of sorrow in his tone broke her heart. "We'd been out shopping, and he collapsed in one of the stores. I called the EMTs, but by the time they got him to the hospital, he was gone. Gina wasn't even a year old then. We'd adopted her at six months, thinking we'd have a lifetime of memories to make together. Then, just like that, I was a single father, trying to raise a baby on my own while also processing my grief. It wasn't a good time for any of us."

"Oh, gosh. I'm so very sorry for your loss," Morgan said, putting her hand over his. "That must've been terrible."

"It was. I tried to keep my restaurant in Seattle open, but my heart wasn't in it after Scott died. I'd grown up on Whidbey Island, and my mother was the chef for Ely's family for years. And I needed to work. Scott had been our breadwinner. He was in finance and made great money at it. But his medical bills ate through our savings after he was gone, and I couldn't be homeless, not with a child to support."

He gave a sad little shrug. "Then Ely stepped in. He'd heard about Scott through people on the island and tracked me down. Offered to pay for everything, too, all the medical bills. Everything. But I couldn't let him do that. I wanted to work. Needed to after losing pretty much everything I loved. I needed to show myself and Gina that I could stand on my own. Have some pride again. So, Ely offered me the head chef job here at Wingate. Room and board, too. He saved my life. He's a good man."

"Wow." She'd wanted to believe that Ely was the man she'd met on the beach all those years ago, but after her arrival here and discovering so much he hadn't told her, her doubts had grown. Hearing Jeremy's story made her think that perhaps he was a decent person after all. And working with him today with their patients had confirmed that, too. The past had been a girlish dream. This was reality. Still, she'd been through too much to defeat her apprehension quite so easily. She tucked her hair behind her ear and sipped more minty, sweet tea, grateful for the warmth on her constricted throat. "That sounds pretty incredible of him."

"It was." Jeremy smiled at her. "He gave me a future, Morgan. Not the one I'd expected to have, but a good one just the same. And if I'd never moved in here, I'd never have met Sam, so…"

He pulled out his phone and showed her a picture of the mysterious younger Malik brother. Tall, muscled, dark haired, handsome, just like Ely. Same dimples, too. God, those dimples. An image of Ely grinning at her from the helicopter earlier flashed into her head, and her stomach fluttered.

Whoops. No. Stop thinking about Ely and his dimples.

Or any other part of him, for that matter. They'd done well together today. She needed to keep that going, not mess it all up by getting personal with him. Personal never worked out well for Morgan. She took a deep breath and passed the phone back to Jeremy, hoping he didn't notice the slight tremble in her fingers. "I look forward to meeting Sam. Will he be coming to the island while I'm here?"

"He's returning for the Halloween ball at the end of the month. It'll be the first time we've seen each other in months. His schedule's so crazy in New York right now, with the merger and everything. He still calls me every night, though. So sweet." Jeremy gave a rapturous sigh. "You'll love him, I'm sure. Oh, and you'll get to meet Raina then, too."

That took Morgan aback. She frowned. "Really?"

From her own experiences with marriages ending, she'd expected Ely's relationship with his ex-wife to be acrimonious, too, but apparently it wasn't, not if the woman returned to Wingate for visits. "Is she here a lot?"

"Once a month or so." Jeremy shrugged. "She and Ely keep things cordial between them. Why?"

"No reason." Morgan frowned into her tea, doing her best to hide her inner turmoil. "Sounds very…modern."

Jeremy snorted. "Why, Morgan Salas. If I didn't know better, I'd think you were jealous."

"What? No." She protested too much, because the uncomfortable niggle inside said he might be right. Which was complete nonsense. She had no right to be jealous about Ely's relationships. They were work colleagues. That's all. His private life was none of her business.

Jeremy laughed. "Seriously, though. If you're curious, his relationship with Raina is friendly, but that's all. And it works for them. They live in completely separate worlds otherwise. Ely's happy here on the island. As a supermodel, Raina's always flying off to some exotic locale for a photo shoot. If it wasn't for Dylan, I honestly don't think they'd ever have ended up together. They wanted very different things in life. But Ely's devoted to keeping the family support there for Dylan's sake, so they make it work."

Interesting. She'd have to ask Ely more about that sometime. Or not. Since it was none of her business, even if it felt like it was.

"Anyway," Jeremy said, patting her arm, "we should go out to dinner one night in Langley, just the two of us. I can show you around the area, introduce you to some people."

"I'd like that."

They set a date, then Morgan headed home. By the time she arrived at the cottage, it was a bit after eight. She got a fire going in the fireplace with the help of detailed instructions left by Mrs. MacIntosh, and had just settled in with a good book and a cup of cocoa, warm and snuggly in her pj's and blanket, when someone knocked on the door. Scowling, she got up to answer, hoping it wasn't something that would mean she'd have to change and go out into the night again. Rain pattered on the roof, and a cold wind blustered against the walls. She shivered and opened the door a crack to find Ely on her porch.

"Hey," Morgan said, surprised. "What are you doing here?"

"Just stopped by to give you an update. Karen and the baby are okay."

"That's great!" She pulled her fleece pj top tighter around her as the wind gusted once more.

"Yeah. They named her Serenity," he chuckled. "Ironic, since her delivery was anything but."

"Right?"

They stood there a beat or two, her fingers twisting in the hem of her pj top to keep busy. An odd mix of anticipation and apprehension fizzed inside her like soda pop. She should ask him in—that would be the polite thing. But it was late and very dark, and it felt weirdly intimate to let him into her cottage just then. She didn't want to give him the wrong idea.

Is it wrong, though?

Of course it was wrong, she chided herself. She didn't want Ely that way anymore, no matter what the shiver up her spine might say. She was just cold, that's all. To prove her point, she stepped back and opened the door wider. "Please, come in. Get warm by the fire."

"Oh, uh…" He hesitated, perhaps as conflicted as her, before the stiff breeze pushed him closer to the threshold. "Well, maybe just for a second. To get warm, like you said. I won't stay long."

She closed the door behind him, catching a whiff of pine and spicy aftershave as he passed her. With him there, his broad frame seemed to take up all the oxygen in the space. For lack of anything better to say, she pointed toward the coffee table. "I was just going to settle in with a book. Can I get you some cocoa?"

"Oh, no. Thanks. The sugar will keep me up."

"Yeah. I get that." She stared down at her stockinged toes, wondering what the hell to talk about now. Morgan watched as he bent slightly to warm his hands near the flames, the fabric of his jacket stretching across his back, revealing the strong muscles beneath, and…oh, boy. Molten warmth pooled low in her belly, and she looked anywhere but at him then. Not helping. Not at all. "So, busy day, huh?"

"Very busy," he said, staring into the flames, the shadows catching the dips and hollows of his high cheekbones before he stood and faced her once more, his expression serious. "Thank you again for performing the surgery so well."

"Happy to do it," Morgan said, her voice quivering slightly as she took a seat and pulled her blanket around her like a shield from all the things she didn't want to feel with him. "And thanks for showing me around with the home visits."

"No problem." He shoved his hands in his pockets, rocking back slightly on his heels. "Can I ask you something?"

Butterflies swarmed inside her then, and her heart lodged somewhere in her throat. "Uh, okay. Sure."

"Great." Ely took a seat on the sofa, catty-corner from her, and rubbed his palms on the legs of his pants like he was nervous, which only ratcheted the bubbling energy pinballing inside her higher. His Adam's apple bobbed as he swallowed, then said, "What's Boston like? I've never been there and always wanted to go."

"What's Boston like"? Seriously? Such a lame question.

He should have left after telling her about the case. That was what he'd intended to do. But no. Now he was sitting on her sofa asking her stupid questions instead of the things he really wanted to know about her, and…

Gah! This was all a mistake. A horrible miscalculation.

Except, the more time Ely spent around Morgan, the more he wanted. Seeing her in action today with the C-section had reminded him of her passion—in work, and in life in general. And while his life was neat and ordered and perfectly wonderful, it lacked passion. He wanted that passion back dearly.

Morgan watched him a moment, apparently as stunned by his silly question as he felt. But he couldn't think of anything intelligent to ask her now that he was here. He, a physician, well respected in his field, had absolutely no game at all where this woman was concerned. Of course it didn't help, either, when his gaze slid downward against his will to her breasts, their outline more pronounced since she'd crossed her arms beneath them, pushing them up and out into that soft fleece top she was wearing. His palms suddenly itched to touch them, cup them, see if they were as plump and full and just the right size like he remembered. He licked his dry lips and glanced away.

No. Stop looking there. Stop it.

And now his lower body was responding

as well, dammit, as the tension inside him grew stronger. Heat climbed his neck from beneath the collar of his white button-down. Maybe she wasn't going to answer. Maybe she sensed the things he was feeling. Maybe she'd kick him out on his butt as he deserved.

Instead, she just gave him an odd look and snuggled down farther in her chair. "Uh, Boston is a nice city. Brutal winters. Not that I saw much of them. I worked in the ER, and it was very busy, so I didn't have much free time."

"Right." His pulse thumped harder against his temples. Now that he couldn't look at her boobs, it seemed that was all he wanted to do. But he couldn't. Nope. He wasn't that type of man, ruled by his desire. Flustered, he asked the next question that popped into his head, which turned out to be the complete wrong one. "Is that where you met your husband?"

Hell.

Morgan's gaze narrowed, and Ely rushed to cover his blunder.

"Sorry. No idea why I asked that."

Stop talking, idiot.

He couldn't. "I mean, I'd like to get to know you better, but…" He swiped a hand through his hair and looked away. "I didn't mean anything by it."

Morgan untucked her legs from beneath her, placing her pink sock–covered feet on the floor. And now he was looking at her toes, wondering what she'd do if he massaged them, kissed them…

What the hell is wrong with me? Leave. Now.

But he couldn't stand up without knocking into her, because she was close now, too close. Close enough for him to catch the scent of her perfume, something floral and sweet and entirely too intoxicating for his liking. He clenched his jaw, a small muscle ticking in his cheek.

"I'm sorry," he said again, because that seemed to be all he could say tonight. Why couldn't he just let it drop? That would be the easy thing to do, but then, nothing was easy with Morgan, and damn if he didn't like it that way. His blood pounded, and his chest burned. He felt more alive than he had in years. Everything seemed sharper, clearer, including that pinch of regret that had never quite gone away where she was concerned, even after a decade apart from her. The one that got away.

And now, sitting in her cozy cottage on a chilly early-October night, the fire wasn't the only thing crackling. The air around them seemed charged with anticipation, expectation, longing.

Or maybe that was just him.

Morgan watched Ely, waited. For a long moment, neither said a word.

Then they both said in unison, "Look…"

He gestured toward her, feeling flushed and frustrated. "Go ahead."

"No, no," she insisted, her knee bumping his. "Sorry. You go."

Ely sighed. "I was going to say it wasn't my intention to hurt you. Now or last time." He hadn't meant to get into all this with her tonight, but it seemed as good a time as any. Full disclosure. "A few days after I got home from our night on the beach, Raina called me. We'd dated awhile in college, nothing too serious, but we'd had sex. And apparently we hadn't been as careful as we'd thought, because she'd gotten pregnant."

"Oh." The ice in Morgan's tone now nearly gave him frostbite. "And were you two together when you slept with me?"

"What? No!" Ely gave her a startled look. Given what she'd been through, he couldn't blame her for jumping to conclusions, but still. It stung. "I'm not a cheater, Morgan. I would never do that. Never. We'd broken up weeks before I ever met you." Stomach hard, he continued, "I made a mess of it all. With you, with her. Everything. But I'd like to start over fresh, if you're willing, to get through the next few weeks as smoothly as possible. What do you say?"

A silent beat passed before Morgan shook her head, her shoulders slumping. "I'm sorry, too, Ely. I promised myself after Ben died, I'd stop punishing myself. Stop being so suspicious of everyone and everything. And yet, here I am, taking it all out on you, just like I said I wouldn't." She snorted. "So, yes. Let's try this again. A fresh start. I'll try to make these next few weeks less stressful between us, too. I'm not saying—"

Before she could finish that sentence, something loud thwacked against the side of the cottage. They both jumped in their seats.

"What the hell was that?" She frowned at the wall across from them.

"No idea." Ely stood. "Stay here while I check."

He walked to the door, only to find Morgan right on his heels, and glanced back at her over his shoulder. "Which part of 'stay here' did you not understand?"

"The part where you give me orders and I obey them."

Her tart answer made him smile. Safety

wasn't a big concern out here on the island, but he'd better check just in case.

"Look, I've got my coat on already, and it's cold. You wait here where it's warm. Be right back." Ely opened the door only to have a blast of frigid wind knock him back a step into Morgan. She squeaked, and he turned around fast. "Are you okay? The storm's gotten worse since I got here, and…"

His voice trailed off as he realized Morgan was mere inches away, blinking up at him, looking as mesmerized as he felt. Neither of them moved. Time slowed as they both leaned closer, closer, so close their lips brushed once, twice, then latched on, kissing. Ely's brain short-circuited as Morgan melted against him, wrapping her arms around his neck. Every cell in his body remembered her—her soft curves, the scent of lilacs from her hair, the taste of sugar on her tongue. The catch of her breath and her mewls of pleasure when he touched her.

Some tiny part of his mind clanged with alarm. He shouldn't be doing this. Not after what they'd just agreed to. But the need roaring in his blood quickly drowned that out. Drowned out all of it except the fact that this was Morgan, the woman he'd thought about, dreamed about, believed he'd never see again.

Now she was here in his arms again, and he couldn't get enough.

His hands drifted down her sides, barely skimming the sides of those breasts he couldn't stop staring at before, his resistance faltering as his fingers reached the hem of her fleece top, grazing her smooth, silky skin beneath…

Morgan shivered and moaned, and Ely's pants felt altogether too tight.

Buzz, buzz, buzz.

The vibrating of her phone jarred them apart, panting. Her blue eyes looked almost black with arousal, and his first urge was to haul her back to him before his logical side kicked in at last. Morgan was on call tonight.

Hell. He had to stop. They weren't kids anymore. They both had other things to consider. He turned away as she answered her phone.

While she talked to whoever was on the other end of the line, he went outside to check the cottage. Nothing there, no damage, thank goodness. Whatever had struck the place was gone now, but he stood in the cold anyway, letting it work its magic on his overheated body. *Deep breaths. Concentrate on boring stuff, like periodic tables and medical insurance codes.* Anything besides Morgan and how wonderful she'd felt against him. Over and over, he breathed until his pulse slowed and his body calmed.

By the time he stepped back inside, Morgan was ending her call by telling the person to schedule an appointment at the clinic the next day.

"Who was that?" he asked, using work to put some much-needed distance between them.

"Mr. Mowrey? Hurt his foot while hiking. I'm going to see him tomorrow."

"George Mowrey? From Langley?" Ely frowned. "He was on the schedule for the clinic today but no-showed. He has a history of untreated type 2 diabetes. I've been on him for a while now to keep regular appointments so we can watch his blood sugar levels, but he isn't compliant. Hates doctors and clinics." He shook his head. "If he's calling now, I'm guessing the problem's worse than he's letting on. Let me know if he doesn't show up."

"Will do."

Awkwardness formed a kiss-size elephant between them. Ely checked his watch. "I should probably get going. I'll see you tomorrow, then."

Morgan stayed where she was, her lips slightly swollen and her cheeks pink. His traitorous fingertips buzzed with the need to touch her again. He clenched his hands in his pockets instead.

"Good night, then." Ely stepped out onto the tiny porch, looking anywhere but at her.

"Night," Morgan called as he shut the door behind him.

Ely walked into the darkness, wondering how on earth he was going to get through the next month without losing his mind—or his heart.

CHAPTER SEVEN

MORGAN STAYED BUSY the next few days, so she had little time to think about that kiss, which was good. If she'd ever worried that being a GP on a small island would be boring, she'd been mistaken. Her schedule was packed, and there were lots of genuine cases to keep her constantly challenged. She didn't see much of Ely, except in passing. He was polite but distant toward her after the other night, and honestly, that was fine. She was attracted to Ely, yes. But she wasn't looking for anything more.

Am I?

That question still churned in her mind as she took a quick break between patients to grab a cup of coffee in the break room. She'd just added cream and sugar when Sandy popped her head in.

"Hey, Dr. Salas. Do you have a minute?" the LPN asked, her expression worried.

"Sure. What's going on?"

"Can you to take a quick look at a patient for me? I'm doing the postpartum wellness checks today for Ely, and one of the mothers isn't doing so good."

"Anything specific?" Morgan followed Sandy out of the break room, coffee in hand.

"More shortness of breath than I'd expect, and she just doesn't look right. My gut says something's wrong. The patient claims it's the flu, but Dr. Greg gave her Tamiflu before he left, and there's been no improvement." They rounded the corner and headed toward the exam rooms. "I'm worried if I let the patient go now, she won't return."

"Of course." Morgan left her coffee at the nurses' station, then walked over to exam room three and pulled the file from the holder on the door and perused the patient's history. She and Sandy went in together, finding an exhausted-looking young woman with a baby in her arms. According to the chart, the patient had three children, including her tiny five-month-old infant.

"Hello, Mrs. Murphy." Morgan smiled. "I'm Dr. Salas. I hear you're not feeling well today."

"I'm fine." But the dark circles under the patient's eyes and the grayish pallor to her complexion told a different story. Her cheeks looked sunken as well, and her clothes practically hung off her body, signaling sudden weight loss, though Morgan wasn't sure if that was from sickness or the normal stress of parenthood. She glanced at the chart again and noted the woman's recent drop in weight.

"Since you're here," Morgan said, unwinding her stethoscope from around her neck, "why don't you let me check you over?"

"I… I really don't…want to be…a bother…" The woman stopped, out of breath, and Morgan and Sandy exchanged a look. "And please…call me… Rita."

"Okay, Rita." Morgan waited for the patient to transfer the infant in her arms to Sandy, then checked Rita's pulse and blood pressure, both of which were normal. "Where's the rest of your family today?"

"A neighbor's looking after my toddler while I came here. The older two are in school. My husband's working, as usual," Rita said, her breathing still too rapid. "I need to get home soon. They can be a handful. It's no wonder I'm so tired."

"Hmm." Morgan listened to the patient's chest. Lots of rattles and congestion. Her concerns spiked. "Do you have a history of asthma or TB, Rita?"

"No." The patient frowned. "Dr. Greg thought I might have a chest infection. He gave me meds."

"Did they help?"

"Not really." Rita shrugged.

"Did you finish the full course of antibiotics?" Morgan checked the file again. From Dr. Greg's notes, it looked like he hadn't been completely sure what he'd been dealing with. He'd wanted to see Rita back in a week, but there was no record that she'd kept that follow-up appointment.

"I did," Rita said. "But like I said, they didn't really do much."

"Why didn't you keep your follow-up appointment?"

The patient looked guilty. "I meant to, but with the kids and my husband's crazy work schedule, I didn't have time."

"Okay." Morgan moved to the patient's side again. "Lie down and let me do an abdominal check."

She palpated the area through the patient's baggy overalls, discovering swelling and distention around the stomach area, even though the patient was rail thin. Not good.

"Have you had any unusual vaginal bleeding or discharge recently?" Morgan asked.

"No. I mean after the baby, it takes a while

for all that to get back to normal, so no. Nothing weird."

Morgan finished going over the patient's full medical history again, then looked over at Sandy. "Could you check if Dr. Malik is back, please? If so, ask him to come in a moment. Thanks."

The nurse handed the baby back to Rita, then left.

"Why do I need to see Dr. Malik?" Rita asked. "I'm fine, really. I just need a good night's sleep. That's all. I seriously don't want to bother anyone."

Unfortunately, Sandy returned moments later sans Ely. "He's still at the hospital in Seattle, but I've got him on hold for you."

"Thanks. Excuse me a second, Rita. I'll be right back." Morgan stepped out into the hall, the sour taste of dread in her mouth. Unfortunately, she was pretty sure she knew what was going on with the patient, but she wanted another opinion. Because if she was right, she needed to arrange further tests, including MRIs and a lumbar puncture.

"Hey, Morgan," Ely said when she took him off hold. "What's going on?"

She quickly gave him a rundown of the patient's history and current symptoms. "My biggest concern is a tumor. She's only twenty-six, with three young kids, but…"

Ely waited a beat, then said, "I'd get a chest X-ray first, see what's happening inside, then wait for those result before going further. I should be back by the time that's done and I can have a look at her, too, for confirmation, okay?"

"Okay." Morgan nodded. "Thanks, Ely."

"No problem. See you soon."

Morgan ordered the X-ray, then returned to the exam room to tell the patient.

"Are you sure I need this today?" Rita coughed, protesting. "Is my insurance going to cover this?"

"Yes, you need it. And yes, your insurance should cover it, since it's medically necessary. I spoke with Dr. Malik, and we'd both like to get this done now so we can see why the antibiotics didn't help. We'll know more after that. If you're ready, I'll walk you over to radiology. It's just down the hall. Or, if you're too tired, I can have Sandy get you a wheelchair." Morgan smiled. "And you've got free babysitting for a little while. Might as well take advantage of it while you can."

"I guess you're right. Fine." Rita slid off the exam table and followed Morgan into the hall. "I can walk. How long do you think it'll take?"

"Not long. Maybe fifteen minutes for the X-ray, then we just have to wait for the results. And you're next in line."

"Okay."

Morgan left the woman in the capable hands of Joan, their radiology tech, then stopped at the front desk just as Ely walked in, looking at his phone, his dark hair tousled. She watched him for a second, weirdly comforted to know he had her back.

He looked up and saw her. "What's happening with your patient?"

"She's in X-ray now." They went to the nurses' station in the back together. "Then we can figure out what's going on with her."

"Yep." He hung his jacket in his office, replacing it with a lab coat with his name embroidered on the chest pocket. "Where's the chart?"

Morgan handed it to him. "I took another full history."

"Good. Let's wait and see what the films show, then."

Half an hour later, they had Rita's films up on the computer, and Morgan's heart sank. Both lungs were dotted with white circles, indicative of cancer. It was even worse than she'd suspected. Poor Rita.

"We need more tests to be sure. A lumbar puncture." Ely scowled at the screen. "Based on the metastases, it's already stage three, possibly stage four. We'll need to get her referred on to an oncologist in Oak Harbor, stat."

"Yep." Morgan's chest felt hollow and caved in. This was bad. So bad. So unfair. Rita was young. A mother. In the prime of her life. "She's got three children. One's a five-month-old. How do I tell her she's got a terminal illness?"

Ely shook his head, his tawny eyes sad as he placed a hand over hers on the counter. "How about we tell her together? I've known Rita for years. Delivered her last two babies. Plus, I'd like to examine her myself. It's a long shot, but…"

She picked up on that thread of hope in his voice. "Why? What are you thinking?"

He took a deep breath. "She's had some vaginal bleeding but dismissed it as normal after pregnancy, right? But it's been five months since she delivered. Her periods should be regular now."

"But she's also breastfeeding." Morgan considered possibilities. "Are you thinking she had the tumor during her last pregnancy and the hormones accelerated its growth?"

"No. But look at these." He pointed at the images on screen again. "They're called cannonball tumors."

"Okay." Morgan still had no idea where he was going with this. Diagnostically, those types of tumors could signal anything from endometrial cancer to ectopic pregnancy. She should know. She'd been screened for them herself, after...

Her throat constricted, and she swallowed hard, shaking it off. "Where are you going with this?"

"Let me examine her again first. I want to order a urine HCG test."

"Choriocarcinoma?" As far as long shots went, that was the longest. The condition was super rare and, with Rita's medical history, unlikely. Given the spread to her lungs, chemo and radiation might not give Rita much more time, but every second she had with her children now would be precious. Morgan did her best to stay objective, but if Karen's case had been hard, this was heartbreaking.

Some of her anguish must've shown on her face, because Ely pulled her aside as the patient returned to the exam room with Sandy. "Hey." He clasped her upper arms gently.

"Let's not get ahead of ourselves. We're still not sure exactly what we're dealing with, okay? If you need to step out, I can handle this myself."

"No," Morgan said, pulling herself together, but still feeling awful inside. "I'm okay. Rita's who we need to focus on here. She's so young. Her life is just starting. This will change everything for her and husband."

As I know only too well.

He rubbed her arms through the sleeves of her lab coat, warming her despite the chill in her blood. "But at least we caught it now and she has a chance to prepare." He waited a beat or two. "Ready?"

"Ready."

They went into the exam room, and Ely ordered the pregnancy test. After Rita gave her sample and Sandy took it to the lab, the patient sat atop the exam table, feeding her baby. The infant sucked contentedly, falling asleep as they watched.

"Well?" Rita reached over to gently put her now-sleeping infant in their carrier. "Can I go?"

"Not yet, I'm afraid." Ely kept his tone gentle. "We need to wait for the urine test results first."

"What? Why?" Rita frowned, looking between Ely and Morgan. Her voice rose, edged with panic. "I'm not sure why you're running that test anyway. I had my tubes tied, Ely. You did it yourself." She scowled, rehooking the strap on her overalls. "Did you find something? We've known each other forever, Ely. Just tell me."

"Your X-ray showed something concerning." He hesitated. "But I'd like to examine you first before I say anything further, okay?"

Rita sighed. "Okay."

"Any unusual lumps or bumps anywhere?" Ely asked as he palpated her abdomen, same as Morgan had done. "Any unusual findings in your monthly breast self-exams?"

"No. Nothing I've noticed."

"Any other symptoms apart from the breathlessness?"

"Nope. Well, except for the tiredness. But I figured that was pretty normal with two kids and a baby." She gave a short laugh, then coughed. "Seriously, though, Ely. I can't be pregnant again. I love my husband, but we're barely making it as it is, and…"

"I don't think you're pregnant," Ely said reassuringly. "But there's a chance it could be something related to that. I won't know for certain until we get the urine test results. In the meantime, relax. Dr. Salas and I will be back shortly to talk again."

Morgan followed him back out into the hallway, just as Sandy returned from the lab.

"The HCG test is strongly positive," the nurse said.

Ely met Morgan's gaze, and a flush of adrenaline zoomed through her system.

"Choriocarcinoma," they said in unison. The rare condition originating in the placental tissue after a pregnancy or miscarriage suddenly became a real possibility for their patient.

The heaviness in Morgan's chest lifted slightly, and she could breathe again. It was still a cancer diagnosis, but for Rita the news was excellent. Those types of tumors responded extremely well to chemotherapy, and she should hopefully make a full recovery. "The hormones in her bloodstream are being produced by the tumor tissue, then, since her tubal ligation was successful."

"Yep." Ely's shoulders sagged with relief. "We'll still need to do additional testing and a biopsy to confirm the diagnosis. Lumbar puncture, too, to confirm it hasn't spread anywhere else. But based on the patient's history, the urine test and the X-rays, I'm confident that's what we're seeing."

Morgan couldn't stop smiling. "Excellent. Thanks for consulting."

"Thanks for asking." Tiny dots of crimson stained his high cheekbones, and Morgan realized he was blushing. The sweetness of it caused an ache in her chest. "Teamwork. Well done."

His gaze flicked to her lips. Morgan's heart did a little flip. *Oh, boy.*

"Come on," he said over the thud of her heartbeat in her ears. "Let's go tell her."

Saturday morning, Ely drove his old truck toward Morgan's cottage. They weren't expected, but he promised he'd take his son out on the boat today and thought maybe Morgan might like to tag along. As he parked to the side of the cottage, behind her sedan, Ely spotted her on the porch, coffee in hand, staring out at the pewter-colored sea.

"Are we going to surprise her, Daddy?" Dylan said in a loud whisper.

"We are." Ely got out and waved to Morgan, who stood now at the edge of the porch, looking far too good for his peace of mind. Even in faded jeans and a dark sweater, she was the sexiest thing he'd ever seen. He helped Dylan and Gina, who was along with them, out, then grabbed a picnic basket Jeremy had packed for them from behind the seats and locked the truck.

It had been a long, hard week at the clinic. They both deserved a break. He'd even gone so far as to call in a favor from a friend at a neighboring clinic to be on call for them so they wouldn't be disturbed. He glanced over at a somewhat subdued Gina and smiled. "Ready to go sailing?"

The little girl looked up at him, clutching her pink bunny tight. She nodded and grinned back at him, two of her front teeth missing.

"Good." He ruffled her wheat-blond hair, then reined Dylan in beside him. The boy had enough energy for ten men and could be quite a handful sometimes. Ely had been the same at his son's age.

The minute they reached the corner of the cottage, Dylan took off running again, this time up onto the porch, where Morgan stood waiting.

"Dr. Salas. Daddy's taking us out in the boat today and he said I could ask you to come, too. If you want." By the time Ely rounded the corner with Gina, his son was bouncing around from foot to foot, arms waving. "Will you come with us, Dr. Salas? Please? We brought fresh orange juice and homemade muffins from Jeremy, too, for breakfast," Dylan said in an excited rush.

"Surprise," Ely said, his tone droll. "Sorry to just show up like this, but he's been on me to take him out and I know you love the water, so… But I completely understand if you have other plans."

"Oh." She glanced at the water in the distance, her expression wistful. He understood. Nothing better than being out on the sea, wind in your hair and the sun on your face. The weather was perfect, too, crisp and bright with a hint of breeze. Morgan looked back at him, hesitating, and for a second Ely feared she'd say no. His level of disappointment shocked him. Scary, that.

He cleared his throat and placed a hand atop Gina's head. The little girl was stuck to his leg like glue. "We should've called first, and…"

"Please, Dr. Salas!" Dylan pleaded, hopping up and down. "Daddy says we need two adults on the boat if Gina comes, too. You have to come. Please. Please, say yes!"

Morgan bit her lip, clearly stifling a laugh. "Well, with an invite like that, how could I refuse?" She glanced at Ely. "What about patient calls? Is cell service good out on the water?"

"Already covered." He explained about his friend in Langley and how he'd made a deal to cover after-hours and weekend patients for them later in the year when one of their colleagues got married in exchange for his buddy covering this weekend. "So we're good to go."

"Great." Morgan headed for her door. "Let me grab a few things and lock up. Be right with you guys." She took her coffee cup back inside, reemerging a few minutes later with a small tote. She held it up and said, "Waterproof poncho, thermos of coffee, wool beanie and a blanket. Anything else I should bring?"

"Just yourself." He took the tote from her in one hand and held the picnic basket in the other.

She locked up the cottage, then followed them down a stone pathway to the bay, where Dr. Greg kept his boat rigged. *The Nightingale* was a pretty thing. Forty feet of cruising pleasure. Tons of deck volume and interior space and fast as a whip, too.

"We'll go out under the engine, then put the sails up once we're clear of the bay," Ely said, offering a hand to Morgan as she boarded, then lifting each of the kids into the boat off the dock. Dylan was already unable to stand still from pure excitement. They got each kid into a life vest, then had them sit on the padded benches. "It's pretty rocky close to shore, and I need more maneuverability than the sails allow. I'll be helmsman if you'll crew?"

"Absolutely," she said, even giving him a jaunty little salute. "Aye, aye, Captain."

And damn if Ely didn't feel a little shudder of pleasure from that.

They put on their own life vests, then Morgan cast off and they were on their way. Ely loved handling *The Nightingale*, steering them smoothly out of the dock and the bay, then into the larger Puget Sound. Being at the tiller always relaxed him, taking away the stresses of the week. He was in his element and grateful for his mirrored aviator sunglasses to hide his gaze, so he could watch Morgan as much as he liked without her knowing. Time slipped away as she sat with the kids, wind ruffling her hair, her smile wide and easy.

Once they were out at sea, they unfurled the sails, working together almost like they'd been a team for ages. Soon they were speeding along. His blood sang, as it always did, with the thrill of being back on the water again. From Morgan's blissful expression, she felt the same. He wondered how long it had been since she'd been out sailing. He doubted she'd had much time with everything else going on.

"Where are we heading?" she yelled across to him after a little while, interrupting his thoughts.

"Marrowstone Island. Thought we'd hike some trails at Fort Flagler, if you're up for it." He pointed toward the land in the distance. "It's an easy walk, even for the kids. We could have a picnic there, too, enjoy the great views. Sound okay?"

"Sounds great." She looked so happy he wanted to hug her. "How fast can this thing go?"

"Fast." Ely chuckled. "But this is the highest speed I'm comfortable going with kids on board. Maybe another time we'll go out by ourselves and see what she can really do."

"Challenge accepted!" Morgan laughed, and the sound washed over him like fine wine, rich and deep and oh, so intoxicating. His pulse skyrocketed, and his mouth dried. If he wasn't careful, he'd fall for her all over again. He looked away fast, concentrating on the water ahead and not the roar of blood in his veins or the sudden tightness in his body that had nothing to do with stress and everything to do with the woman sitting across the deck from him.

Before long, they sailed into a sheltered cove and lowered the sails. Ely took them to shore under the engine. Without the wind, sunlight prickled hot on his skin, and he tugged off his sweater, leaving him in his T-shirt. Morgan did the same, and his mouth dried to cotton as he took in her tank top, how the thin fabric clung to her body, leaving little to the imagination while covering everything at the same time. More flashes of their night on the beach cranked his internal temperature to boiling—the way she'd arched and moaned as he teased her taut pink nipples...

Not helping, dude. Not at all.

Flustered and frustrated, Ely turned the tiller over to Morgan, then he leaped off the boat onto nearby rocks to anchor them securely. "The tide will be on its way out by the time we get back," he said, not daring to look at Morgan again. "We'll be able to wade out then. In the meantime, start passing the kids across to me, please."

"I can jump!" Dylan yelled, defiant. "I'm not a baby anymore."

"These rocks are slippery, son," Ely said in the same tone his dad used to use with him. The one that brooked no argument. "On the boat, you always do exactly what the captain says. No argument."

Morgan bit back another grin and handed Gina over, then turned to pick up Dylan. The kid sighed but allowed it. Ely shook his head. His son sure knew how to be dramatic when needed. He'd gotten that from his mother. Yep.

"Wait for us just up the hill there, kids." Ely held out his hand out to Morgan. She grabbed her tote bag from him, the touch of their fingers sending zings of pure desire up his arm as she leaped onto the rocks beside him. For a brief second, they were chest to chest, heartbeat to heartbeat. He'd swear hers was racing as fast as his. Their eyes locked, held. It was too much and not enough all at once. He squeezed her hand tighter, tugging her closer, closer…

A seagull squawked loud, diving into the water nearby and splashing them both. Reality snapped back. He cleared his throat and let Morgan go, moving aside to let her pass, his entire body vibrating like a tuning fork because of her.

Walking helped. They followed the trails at an easy pace, letting the kids run on ahead. Partway up to the summit, they stopped for a break. Even with the breeze, it was hot, and perspiration slicked his forehead. Ely used the hem of his T-shirt to wipe his face, not missing how Morgan stared at his bare abs. His skin tingled, like she'd touched him, and now all he could think about was her stroking him there, moving upward over his pecs, tickling through his chest hair. And now heat of a different kind flooded his system.

Enough resting for now.

To keep the kids in sight as they climbed uphill, Ely lengthened his stride, and Morgan fell back a bit. They didn't talk much, which was fine, since he wasn't sure he had enough oxygen for that anyway. Usually, these trails were easy for him. But today, he was having a hard time. Probably because his body was too busy lusting after the woman beside him.

When they finally reached a clearing at the top, Morgan stopped in her tracks, gasping. "That view is spectacular."

The summit wasn't particularly high, but you could look out over Puget Sound and Whidbey Island in the distance—all lush green grass and blue skies and wildflowers.

"You should check out Camano Island while you're here," he said from beside her. "The San Juan Islands, too, up north. They're all beautiful and have their unique sights to see."

"I'll try. Thanks." Morgan shaded her eyes with her hand as she looked up at him. "Maybe we could take the boat up there some weekend, unless you think Dr. Greg would mind."

"Maybe," Ely managed to say past his tight vocal cords. Spending more time alone with Morgan on the boat would be a fantasy come true. A very erotic fantasy. He swallowed hard. "October can be a tricky month, weatherwise. It can be beautiful one minute and awful the next. The coast guard are always having to rescue hapless tourists this time of year. I'd hate for anything to happen. We need you at the clinic. I need…" He stopped, realizing how close they were standing now. How did they get so close? He stared into her eyes, and his gums thudded in time with his pulse. "I…uh…"

Get it out…

Nope. He turned toward the horizon again. "I need you at the practice, is what I was trying to say. With Dr. Greg gone."

Lame, dude. So lame.

Needing to get away before he made an even bigger fool of himself, he grabbed the first excuse that popped into his head. "I should check on the kids."

Morgan's stare prickled the back of his neck as he headed off in the direction of his son and Gina. God. Why did he become a blathering idiot around her? It wasn't like they were virgins. Hell, it wasn't even the first time they'd slept together. Maybe he was just out of practice. Or maybe it was because he liked things calm, cool, collected. Predictable. And being around Morgan, things were anything but predictable.

Dylan ran around with Gina in the meadow in front of him, playing tag and laughing.

Then it hit him, like a cartoon anvil right on the head.

Right there. That was why he had to be careful.

His son was the most important thing in the world to him. He needed to stay focused on Dylan and forget the rest. He shouldn't need love or passion or romance. The coparenting situation with his ex-wife wasn't ideal, and yes, he got lonely sometimes, but it worked for them. It was a known variable. Morgan was not. Her stint here was done at the end of the month, and she could fly off to Africa again or even Antarctica, for all he knew. And yes, she'd said she wanted a quieter, peaceful life going forward, but that didn't necessarily include him or his son. No. He couldn't take that risk.

"Yay! Muffin time. I'm starving!" Dylan ran past him to where Morgan had started laying out the blanket and the food. "Daddy, can we eat now?"

"Yep." Ely retuned to the blanket and plopped down on one side, opening one of the containers Jeremy had packed for them. "What kind of muffin do you want, son? Blueberry or cranberry?"

"Blueberry!" Dylan sat beside Morgan, and Ely put a muffin on a plate, then handed it to Dylan, along with a napkin. "Thanks, Daddy!"

"Sure." Ely looked to Gina. "What about you? Ready for a muffin?"

"Yes, please," the little girl said. "Cranberry. My daddy makes the best muffins."

"He sure does." Ely got a plate ready for Gina. "What about drinks? Looks like we've got a couple juice boxes in here or bottled waters."

"Juice box!" Gina and Dylan yelled in unison.

"Guess that leaves us with the waters, huh?" Morgan snorted, jamming a straw into the top of each juice box for the kids, then taking the water Ely handed her. He was careful not to let their fingers touch this time. If she noticed, Morgan didn't say anything.

Once they were all eating, Dylan carried the conversation, chattering away about his schoolwork and the kids in class and his favorite subjects, history and science, just like his dad.

After they'd all finished and the kids went back to playing, Ely stood and scanned the sky. "Clouds are rolling in from the north. Might be bad weather coming. We should go. Wouldn't want to get stuck here during a storm, and the tide will be going out anyway."

Morgan gave him a skeptical look. "Really? It seems so nice out."

"I grew up here. Trust me." Then, realizing what he'd said, he glanced her way as he started packing up their stuff. "Or don't. Trust me, I mean."

She chuckled and gave him a reluctant smile. "I do. Trust you. At least about the weather."

Her words made him feel ten feet tall. By the time they made it back down to the shore, the tide was on the way out, as he'd predicted, dragging *The Nightingale* with it. Now there was an expanse of shallow water and sand to cross where there'd been several feet of sea before. He and Morgan rolled up their jeans and waded out. He tried not to notice her shapely, tanned calves or her cute bare feet with their pink toenails. Yep. Just as he'd thought, those toes were very kissable indeed.

"Kids, stay on shore and wait for me. I'll be back to get you. Understand?"

Both kids nodded, already working on a sandcastle.

About halfway to the boat, the water got deeper fast. Soon it was up to Ely's waist and Morgan's chest. He stopped and looked at Morgan, careful not to let his gaze dip to her now see-through tank top. "Let me carry you the rest of the way."

"No." Morgan backed away slightly. "I'm fine. In fact, you go back and get Dylan and Gina. I can make it the rest of the way to the boat on my own."

"Don't be silly." He scowled and scooped her up in his arms, despite her protests. "Crew all gets treated the same. Captain's orders." He hoisted her higher against his chest and continued toward the boat, digging his toes into the sandy sea bottom to keep stable. Waves battered against him, splashing up his chest and into his face, but all Ely could seem to concentrate on was how soft Morgan's curves felt pressed to his chest, the warmth of her breath over his skin drowning out the salt and the sea and all his fears and doubts. His swim trunks grew uncomfortably tight despite the icy water.

Oh, God.

Distracted, he stubbed his toe on a rock beneath the water, and everything went topsy-turvy. One second, they were standing upright. The next, Ely tipped forward. He tried to hang on to Morgan, but it was too late. They went under. Water gurgled in his ears as he surfaced, choking and gasping, to find Morgan across from him, doing the same, her hair slicked back and her eyes glinting with humor.

Well, that was one way to distract himself, he supposed.

They swam against the current the last several feet to the boat, and he helped her up onto the ladder so she could climb aboard. Morgan flopped down onto the deck like a landed fish, then clambered to her knees, a piece of seaweed stuck to the front of her wet tank top, right between her taut nipples. Her cheeks were flushed, and her blue eyes sparkled with something more than humor now. Something darker and a whole lot more exciting.

Ely swallowed so hard it clicked in his ears, then returned to shore fast for Dylan and Gina, praying the cold water would work its magic on his overheated libido.

By the time he got the kids into the boat, one tucked under each arm, Morgan seemed to have regained some of her composure, too.

He cast them off from the rocks, then climbed the ladder himself.

"Are there any towels?" Morgan asked, pulling another bit of seaweed from her hair and tossing it over the side.

"Check below." Ely pulled off his sodden shirt. "Take the kids with you. It's probably warmer down there anyway."

"What about you?" she asked.

"I'm fine." He turned away to start the engine.

"Okay," Morgan said, heading down the stairs below decks. "Be right back. Come on, kids."

"There's a small gas stove down there, too," he called from behind them. "Maybe there's cocoa."

Cocoa was the last thing on Ely's mind, though. He was concerned about control and the fact that he was losing the battle to maintain it when it came to Morgan. Even more concerning was the fact he liked it. Liked feeling reckless and wild and free with her. And that scared him most of all.

CHAPTER EIGHT

BY THE TIME they arrived back at the bay in front of Morgan's cottage, the wind had picked up considerably. Dark clouds scudded across the sky as the first drops of rain fell. Ely had been right to cut their trip short after all. Morgan tidied the boat, then stood on deck, ready to jump out with the ropes to fasten *The Nightingale* to shore. As she did, she noticed a figure waiting atop the hill for them. Not Jeremy. This person looked to be female. Huh. A patient, maybe?

The mysterious arrival's identity was soon confirmed, however, when Dylan got ashore and quickly ran up the hill. "Mommy! Wait till you hear what happened. Daddy tried to carry Dr. Salas to the boat and they both fell in the water. And she had seaweed in her hair and we had muffins and juice. I wish you came with us."

Great. Not exactly an ideal way to meet the

ex, with Morgan looking like a drowned rat and wearing someone else's sweater because her own clothes were soaked. Didn't matter. She wasn't trying to impress anyone, right? Still, she couldn't stop herself from tugging at the hem of the sweater, now hanging unevenly to her knees, as she stared at Ely's supermodel ex in front of her.

And honestly, the fabled Raina looked pretty much exactly like Morgan had expected her to—tall, thin, with long blond hair and sea foam–green eyes, the same as Dylan's. She was dressed immaculately, too, like she'd walked right out of a Ralph Lauren ad, only serving to make Morgan feel more like a soggy slug. The woman's smile was nothing but friendly, though, as she stepped forward to shake Morgan's hand, and now Morgan felt bad for being ungracious.

"I hope Dylan wasn't too much trouble today. Jeremy sent me down to invite you all for dinner at Wingate." She fiddled with Gina's braids, then looked over at Ely, who'd finally joined them. "I have to go back to Paris tomorrow for fashion week. But I'll be back in time for the ball at the end of the month."

Dylan's lower lip trembled as he clung to his mother's leg. "Do you have to go, Mommy?

Can't you stay for a while this time?" He turned to Ely. "Daddy, tell her to stay."

Ely sighed and shook his head. "Your mom has to work, son."

"I hate work. Stupid Paris." Dejected, Dylan stalked off toward the truck alone, head bowed and little shoulders bent. Morgan's heart ached for him.

Ely looked from his son to Raina, frowning. "You did tell him you were staying awhile this time."

"I know. I'm sorry. But one of the top designers had a last-minute cancellation with another model, and my agent got me booked into the spot. It's a lot of money." She sighed, crossing her arms. "We've had this conversation, Ely. You know I love Dylan, and I'm sorry to disappoint our son this time, but he'll get over it. I'll bring him back something nice, too, as a present."

"Gifts don't make up for quality time," Ely grumbled.

The air chilled, and not because of the approaching storm. Morgan did her best to inch toward the cottage. This wasn't her business, no matter how curious she might be.

Finally, Raina said, "I'll stay longer at the end of the month. Besides, Dylan's in school now. He won't miss me as much."

"Yes, he will. He always does when you're gone." Ely started to his truck with Gina as thunder rolled in the distance.

Raina turned her attention back to Morgan. "I'm sorry. But enough about that. Can I let Jeremy know you'll be joining us, Morgan?" she asked, pleasant as could be, like she and Ely hadn't just been having a polite disagreement.

"Oh, um." She pulled the baggy sweater tighter around herself. "No, actually. I think I'm just going to take a nice hot bath then watch a movie. Maybe another time." She waved to Ely and the kids, who were waiting by the truck. "It was nice to meet you."

"Same." Raina smiled, then turned toward the Mercedes parked near Ely's truck.

"Does that mean we can do it again?" Dylan yelled back at Morgan from the truck window, his expression brightening once more.

"Anytime," Morgan called back. "Ask your dad, and if I'm free, we'll take a picnic and go."

Once they'd all left, Morgan went inside and quickly showered and changed before making herself dinner then climbing under a blanket on the sofa. By then, the storms had arrived full force. The windows rattled against the onslaught of rain and wind.

Morgan tried to read a book, but the creak of the roof kept distracting her. She shuddered. At least she wasn't on call tonight. The lights flickered once or twice but thankfully stayed on. Morgan tucked her feet under her and snuggled deeper under her warm blanket, only to jump at a knock on the door.

Who in the world would be out in this?

Ely, apparently. He stood on her threshold, hair plastered to his forehead and completely soaked. "Sorry to ask on a night like this, but I need your help. One of the local fishing boats didn't return this evening. Coast guard search and rescue are sending a helicopter since it's too rough for a lifeboat. I'm going up with the flight crew. We'll need all staff at the clinic if we find them. Langley's sending people over, too, just in case. There were four men on that boat." His voice cracked with anguish. "I know them all."

"Oh, no." Her pulse tripped, and her chest constricted. "Let me get dressed. You should've just phoned and saved the trip. I would've gone straight to the clinic."

"Service is down again. It's usually the first thing to go during storms this bad." He took a deep breath and stared longingly at the fireplace. "And I didn't want you driving to the clinic on your own. High tide's coming in, and some of the bridges are already washed over. It's easy to get lost. You can follow me. I need to be ready to go the minute the chopper gets to the clinic."

"Okay. Just give me a minute."

Once she was ready, they made their slow way toward the clinic. Morgan gripped the steering wheel tight, nails digging into her palms. Even with the wipers on high, she could barely see the road in front of her, following Ely's taillights instead to stay oriented. They crossed a small bridge, and water splashed against the side of her sedan. For one horrifying second, Morgan feared she'd be swept out to sea, and her stomach plummeted. Finally, after what seemed a small eternity, they reached the clinic.

"Any sign of the coast guard chopper yet?" Ely asked the rest of the staff once they were inside.

"They haven't been able to take off yet," Sandy said from her post at a two-way radio. "Waiting for another crew member and for the wind to die down."

Ely cursed under his breath. "The longer those men are out there, the less chance they have."

"Coast guard crew on the radio," Sandy said, handing him the receiver.

Everyone listened in silence as he spoke with them. Morgan couldn't hear what was said, but based on Ely's grim expression, it wasn't good. At last, he replaced the receiver and turned to the anxious group.

"More trouble, I'm afraid. A tourist's car went over the side of one of the bridges. It isn't submerged yet, but the driver is trapped, and the tide is rising. The fire department is on scene. They're requesting medical assistance. EMTs are all busy on other calls. They may have to cut the driver out of the vehicle. I'm going to go. Didi, can you get my medical kit?"

"Let me do it, Ely," Morgan offered. "You wait here for the helicopter."

He shook his head. "Based on what the coast guard said, it'll be at least an hour before they arrive."

"Then at least let me come with you." She might not be as familiar with the area, but she wasn't going to just sit by and do nothing while people's lives were in danger. "I'll need a medical kit, too, Didi."

Ely hesitated then exhaled slow. "Are you sure? It could get dangerous."

"All the more reason for me to go, then."

He seemed to come to a decision and gave a curt nod. "Fine. We'll take my truck. It's got four-wheel drive."

They braved the lashing rain once more on the way to Ely's vehicle. The air temperatures weren't particularly cold, but the chilly waters of Puget Sound could bring on hypothermia and death within minutes this time of year. Travel was slow again, but they found the bridge where the tourist accident had occurred, mainly by letting the flashing red and blue lights guide them.

"Any luck, Drew?" Ely called to one of the firemen as they got out and approached the partially submerged vehicle.

"Not yet," the burly guy said. "Four people in the car—husband, wife, two kids. So far, we've got everyone out except the husband. His foot's stuck on something in there, and the tide is rising. Water's up to his shoulders now, and he's panicking."

"Any chance to pull the car out, occupant and all?" Ely asked, squinting down at the scene.

"Already tried, but it didn't work," the firefighter said. "If we had more time, maybe. But I'm guessing all we have is ten, maybe fifteen minutes before the car's submerged completely."

"Best take a look, then." Ely slid down the embankment and into the churning water surrounding the car. The eerie glow of the vehicle's submerged headlights rippled around his hips as he peered inside the vehicle, trying to find what was trapping the driver's foot in the car. Morgan knew that if they couldn't get him unstuck, they might be forced to amputate just to save his life. She'd seen it happen before, in Africa. Her pulse stumbled. But they couldn't let the man drown, either.

Determined to help as much as she could, she skidded down the slope, too, on the opposite side of the car from Ely, holding her medical kit above her head to keep it dry. Drew, the burly firefighter, followed close behind her. She reached the passenger side door and stuck her head in through the shattered window to speak to the terrified driver.

"Sir, I'm Dr. Salas. What's your name?"

"B-Bob," the man said between chattering teeth. "B-Bob Taylor."

"Well, Mr. Taylor, we're here to get you out. Please try to stay calm and this will all be over soon." Through the windshield, Morgan saw Ely toss his med pack atop the hood, then dive below the water. Her breath froze until he resurfaced a few moments later.

"It's murky down there," Ely called, water

sluicing down his face. "Too hard to see. Sir, can you feel where your foot is stuck?"

"I—I'm n-not s-sure. I th-think m-maybe under the gas pedal," the man said.

"Could we pull him out if all three of us tried at once?" Morgan offered, looking from Ely to the firefighter beside her side.

"No. Too risky," Ely said. "We could injure him more that way. Let me look again on this side."

He dived below the freezing water once more. Morgan had been standing there only a few minutes, and her feet were already going numb. She couldn't imagine how miserable poor Mr. Taylor must be. To make matters worse, the car was teetering precariously on the rocks. Any slight bump or disruption could send it sliding deeper into the water, taking Mr. Taylor—and possibly Ely—with it.

The weight on her chest intensified, making her breaths shallower.

The clock ticked.

The victim looked paler now, and his lips were turning blue, sure signs of impending shock. Morgan propped her medical kit on the edge of the window and pulled out an oxygen mask. She handed the cylinder to the fireman beside her to hold, then carefully reached past the shards of broken glass to slip the mask over the man's face, using her calmest voice. "This will help you breathe until we can give you something for the pain, okay?"

An unholy screech of metal on rock sounded, and the car jerked downward. Her stomach lurched as the fireman stepped back, pulling Morgan with him. *Ely.* Where was Ely? For an awful second, she thought the vehicle might disappear completely into the choppy waves, but thankfully it stopped after a few inches. Morgan inched closer again, and through the open window, she held Mr. Taylor's hand as she searched the frothing waters around them for Ely. Hot bile scalded her throat. No sign of him.

Please let him be okay. I can't lose him. There's so much left to say, so much left undone...

He surfaced then, a few feet away, and relief so profound her knees nearly buckled washed over Morgan. She wanted to run and throw her arms around him, but she needed to stay with their patient.

"Whew. That was close." Ely spit out a mouthful of water. Instead of terror on his face, though, he looked energized. Like he enjoyed the danger. "I got a better look inside the driver's side foot well, and I think we can get him out if one of you pulls while

I maneuver his ankle out from beneath the gas pedal." Then he said to Mr. Taylor, "Sir, your ankle is broken. We'll get you out, but it'll be painful."

Mr. Taylor let go of Morgan's hand to lower his oxygen mask. "I don't care. Just help me."

Gusts screeched like banshees through the night, and Morgan reached back into the medical kit. "Let me give him a shot of morphine. That should take the edge off while we get him unstuck." She pulled out a prefilled syringe and uncapped it with her teeth. With any luck, the guy would pass out completely and save himself the suffering.

Meds given, they got to work. Ely went back underwater to lift the gas pedal while Morgan held the car door and the burly firefighter pulled Mr. Taylor to safety. They got him out just in time, too, as the water began to overtake the engine block and the headlights winked out. Morgan felt like she was in an action-adventure movie. Except the chill in her bones told her this was all too real. She wasn't sure she'd ever be warm again.

Ely was shaking uncontrollably, too, when he joined her a few minutes later. They both huddled under thermal blankets while they waited beside Mr. Taylor's gurney for the ambulance to arrive.

"M-my f-family?" Mr. Taylor asked. "Are they all right, too?"

"Yes. One of the firefighters has driven them to the clinic to be checked over," Morgan said once her teeth stopped chattering, doing her best to soothe the man as the EMTs finally pulled up. "Don't worry. It's only a precaution. They're fine. We promised you'd be right behind them."

"Thank you," Mr. Taylor said, his words a bit slurred from the morphine before he drifted off again.

"You ride with him," Ely said to Morgan as they loaded the patient into the back of the rig. "I'll drive back myself."

He took off for his truck before Morgan could answer, looking entirely in his element. She climbed in beside Mr. Taylor for the ride to the clinic. When they got there, the place was a hive of activity. The man's family huddled in the waiting room, looking bedraggled and shocked but otherwise fine, according to Sandy. Still in his wet clothes, Ely got back on the radio again.

"The helicopter still can't take off," he said a few minutes later when Morgan joined him. "Another trawler spotted our disabled boat, though. It's still afloat, but limping. They couldn't get too close because of the choppy water, but there's still hope the crew is all right. For now, all we can do is wait."

"Go get changed, both of you." Sandy shooed them away from behind the counter. "You're dripping all over my nice clean floor." Despite her cross tone, the nurse's concern was obvious. "Mr. Taylor's in X-ray now, and depending on the severity of the fracture, we'll either set it for him or send him on to Oak Harbor after the storm is over. For now, they stay put. No one should go back out in this."

Morgan changed into a clean pair of scrubs and socks she'd found in the changing room. When she returned to the desk, Sandy thrust a steaming cup of coffee into her hands. She'd never felt such bone-deep weariness in her life, and the night wasn't even over yet. She slumped into a chair at the nurses' station and closed her eyes, letting the warmth from the mug in her hands seep into her bones.

She must've dozed a bit, though, because the next time she opened her eyes, Morgan noticed the wind had quieted, and the rain had slowed to a patter. Ely sat beside her, having changed into scrubs, too.

"What's happening?" she asked him around a yawn.

"Coast guard's taking off now." He raked

a hand through his tousled hair. "They'll be here in about twenty minutes. They've reestablished contact with the fishing boat, and according to reports, one of the crew has a suspected head injury. I'll go down to the boat to make an assessment."

Faint lines around his eyes and mouth stood out in sharper contrast, and dark circles shadowed his eyes. Dark stubble covered his jaw, and there was a tiny cut on one of his cheeks.

"Maybe I should go instead of you," she offered. "At least I've had a nap."

"I'll be okay." Ely flashed a lopsided grin, showing off those dimples of his again. She wanted to hug him and tell him everything would be all right, even if it wouldn't. "I volunteer with the local rescue team, so I've been trained for this."

"Hey," she said, frowning. "I thought we were a team here. There's plenty of people here at the clinic. I want to go with you, in case you need backup."

He seemed to consider that a moment, looked like he wanted to argue, but then exhaled slow. "I just don't want anything to happen to you, Morgan. I'd never forgive myself if…"

She took his hand and squeezed, her gaze earnest. "And you don't think I feel the same?"

They looked into each other's eyes a long moment, and a silent understanding passed between them.

"Okay," Ely said, kissing the back of her hand quick. "Let's go."

They pulled on dry coats and went outside to the open field to wait for the chopper to land. Ely introduced her to the crew while they put on their flight suits and harnesses. "This is Dr. Salas. She'll be my medical backup."

The crewman nodded, making final adjustments to Morgan's harness. "Been in a helicopter before?"

"No," she said. "But I love flying."

The crewman handed her a set of headphones, shouting over the roar of the rotors. "Gets pretty loud up there. You'll need these. I have to warn you, it's going to be a bumpy ride."

Morgan glanced over at Ely. He looked perfectly at home, like he'd been doing this all his life. Maybe he had. He gave her a thumbs-up, his obvious excitement infectious. Then he made a slight adjustment to her helmet, his fingers brushing her skin and making her tingle from more than anticipation.

"Last chance to change your mind," Ely

said into his mic. The words reverberated in her headphones.

"No way." She climbed into the helicopter ahead of him. "We've got patients to save."

And yep. It was turbulent as hell in the air, just as the crewman had warned. The chopper lurched and dropped, and despite her bravado, Morgan held tight to Ely's leg, squeezing her eyes closed. When she dared open them again, she found him watching her, his expression amused.

"Okay?" he asked through the mic, laughing.

Embarrassed, she nodded, uncurling her fingers from his thigh, but the feel of his rock-hard muscles lingered in her mind, despite more pressing issues ahead. "Fine."

"When we get to the boat, they'll lower me down," Ely explained as they neared the site of the stricken boat. "I'll make the assessment on the head injury. Meanwhile, they'll send down a basket to lift the rest of the stranded crew to safety. Once the other men are on-board, you'll need to triage them for treatment."

"Got it." Morgan gave him a thumbs-up. "Or should I say 'Roger'? Like they do in the movies?"

Ely grinned, and there were those darned

dimples again. Thankfully, the pilot interrupted before she could get too distracted, announcing they'd reached their destination. Morgan peered out the side of the chopper at the rain-streaked gray water below, but didn't see the disabled vessel. Then Ely directed her attention to a point forward from where she was looking, and she made out the vague shape of a listing boat, just large enough for the four-man crew and their catch. Three fishermen in bright yellow slickers stood on deck, waving their arms frantically. The absent fourth fisherman was the one to worry about.

As the helicopter hovered over the scene, Ely made his final preparations to be winched down.

She watched, chest constricted, as the cable lowering him swayed in the wind. The fishing boat was also moving with the waves, making the landing tricky. If not for the skill of their pilot, they could crash, or Ely could be crushed. Luckily, he made it onboard, giving them an A-OK salute before unhooking from the cable. Then the next part of the process began.

A few heart-stopping minutes later, the first fisherman arrived in the chopper. Morgan and a crewman pulled him on board, where the man lay gasping and shivering on the floor. She had enough time to do a brief check on him—cold and shocked but otherwise unharmed—before the next fisherman arrived.

The second man pulled on her sleeve to get her attention. "It's Jack who's hurt," he rasped. "The rest of us are all right. But Jack got hit on the back of the head by the winch. He's in a bad way."

"Don't worry," Morgan said, returning her attention to examining him. "Ely will look after him."

"I don't think Jack can move," the first man said. "Hasn't moved since the accident."

Satisfied the second fisherman was unhurt as well, Morgan moved on to the third man, who'd just arrived. Her mind raced with the new information. If the fourth fisherman had sustained an injury to his brain or spinal cord, things would become much more complicated.

Sure enough, Ely confirmed the worst by radio a few minutes later.

"Probable spinal fracture. I can't risk moving him. You'll have to leave me here for now."

"Roger that," the pilot replied. "Can you stay afloat until we can get you towed in?"

"I think so." Ely sounded less sure now, and Morgan's chest squeezed tight. "I need to go silent for a few minutes so I can listen to Jack's chest. Be back online when I'm done."

The third fisherman shouted something Morgan couldn't make out, but she could tell from the man's expression he was worried. She knew how he felt.

"What is it?" she asked.

"Ely hit his head going below to check on Jack," the fisherman said. "Nasty cut on his forehead."

Head injuries were nothing to mess with. If Ely passed out, the boat could get lost in the current or sink. Morgan grabbed the cable and hooked it to her harness. "I need to go down and help Ely."

"Sorry, ma'am." The coast guard crewman stopped her. "It's too dangerous for untrained civilians."

Jaw set, Morgan gave him the same look she'd used on belligerent patients in her ER back in Boston, the one that usually put the fear of God into them. "I'm not an untrained civilian. I'm an experienced sailor as well as a doctor. And it's my duty to help those in need."

Her fierce tone gave the guy pause, and he glanced at the pilot. "What do you think?"

"I don't like it, but if we're going to drop her down, we need to do it now. Fuel's low."

"Are you sure?" the crewman asked, and Morgan nodded. "Okay. Let's get you on that ship."

She kept her eyes closed tight as she was lowered, truly scared for the first time. The rope swayed with the combined turbulence of the helicopter's blades and the wind, and her stomach lurched. Ely would be furious, but she didn't care. Better him angry now and alive than dead in Puget Sound.

Sure enough, when she touched down on the deck, Ely ran up to her, unhooking her cable, seemingly oblivious to the blood streaming down his face from the gash on his forehead. The chopper flew away, leaving them alone on the stranded, disabled vessel.

"What the hell are you thinking, Morgan? Now you're trapped here."

"I'm not trapped. You need help, Ely. You can't care for your patient properly if you're hurt yourself," she said, gesturing toward his forehead as she set her medical kit down at her feet. "Teamwork, remember?"

The boat rocked precariously. With each wave, they took on more water, making it list even more. From experience, Morgan knew they needed to turn into the wind to avoid capsizing, then keep the boat on that course until they reached shore. A calm descended over her. Water had never frightened her. Treat it with respect and keep calm and you'd be fine. Besides, someone had to steer this thing until help arrived, and Ely needed to stay with his patient belowdecks. She told him as much. "Go back below. I'll stay here at the helm. If you need help, let me know. You should let me look at that cut, too."

Two hours crept by. Every now and then Ely would check on her, and she noticed he'd at least put a bandage on his forehead. Good. Eventually the rain and wind eased, and visibility improved. A lifeboat came toward them. She yelled to let Ely know, and as soon they were secured to the stable vessel, she went below. Ely sat beside Jack, looking bedraggled and in pain. She crouched beside him to carefully examine his forehead without undoing the bandage and risking the wound bleeding again.

"You want some analgesics?" she asked him.

"Nah." Ely gave her a tired smile. "Need to stay alert for Jack. I'll take something later."

Another hour passed before they were back on dry land. The air ambulance stood ready to transfer Jack to a neurosurgeon at Seattle

General, although he'd begun to rouse and use his limbs again, which was a positive sign. Hopefully, there'd be no lasting damage.

Once they were back at the clinic, Ely reluctantly agreed to let Morgan suture his wound.

"Are you sure you're not too tired?" He looked at her, gaze narrowed.

"I'm more alert than you are." That seemed to shut him up, and he let her close the wound, flinching slightly when she injected the lidocaine. "And you're welcome for saving your butt today."

Ely held his breath, and for a moment, she thought maybe she'd gone too far. They were both exhausted and she'd let her emotions get the best of her there, but dammit. She'd been so scared for him. If he'd gotten badly hurt or worse… Her head spun just thinking about it. She concentrated on her stitches, neat and even and tight. He wouldn't even have a scar.

"I'm sorry. You're right. You were fantastic out there, Morgan," he said. "And I couldn't have done it without you. I just wish you hadn't put yourself at risk to help."

She tied off the last stitch then sat back, frowning. "We're partners, remember?"

"But I don't… I can't…" He leaned forward, rubbing a hand over his face, careful to avoid the area she'd just worked on. "Since my parents were killed in a plane crash, I've been terrified of losing control. Of losing the people I care for. I never want to go through that again. But I can't control you, Morgan. You scare the hell out of me, because I care. Way more than I should, and if anything happened to you today, I can't… I wouldn't…"

His voice trailed off as he hung his head, and Morgan blinked, taking that in. He cared. She cared, too. Way more than she'd intended, and whoa. That was scary. Way scarier than any water rescue could ever be.

In the end, she cleared her throat around the odd sudden lump of longing lodged there, her eyes getting misty as she grabbed clean gauze pads and bandages to finish patching him up. Morgan was glad she was facing away from him as she said huskily, "I'm sorry that happened to you, Ely. I wouldn't want to cause you any additional pain."

I care about you, too.

It had been so long since she'd allowed herself to be open and vulnerable like that, and it left her feeling raw and achy inside.

When she turned back around, Ely caught her hand, bringing it to his lips, and her heart stuttered. "Thank you, Morgan. For everything. It means the world to me."

And just like that, all her good intentions about keeping her distance, keeping things professional, went right out the window. It was a good thing she was sitting down, because otherwise she probably would've melted into a puddle of goo at his feet. That was possibly the sweetest thing anyone had ever said to her.

And while she was terrified, she also now felt...hopeful.

By the time they left the clinic, the sun was rising. The wind had died down to a gentle breeze, and it promised to be a fine day ahead. Morgan was so tired, though, she probably wouldn't see most of it and she certainly didn't feel awake enough to drive. So, she arranged with another staff member to dive her vehicle back to her cottage later, then accepted Ely's offer of a ride home. She planned a warm bath, a hot meal, then bed. Not necessarily in that order. In fact, they'd barely left the parking lot before she fell asleep in the passenger seat of Ely's truck.

She woke to the sensation of being lifted, her head cradled against a solid, warm chest as she was carried inside her cottage and lowered onto her bed. She wanted to reach out, say something, but she didn't have the energy. Just before she gave in to sleep once more, Ely kissed her temple, his lips light as a feather. "Sleep tight, *janaan*."

The sound of him leaving barely registered as she fell into a deep sleep.

CHAPTER NINE

DESPITE THE BUSY NIGHT, Morgan woke at her usual early time. After dressing, she checked her phone, relieved to find she had service again. Sandy had texted that all the patients from the clinic last night were doing well and not to worry about coming in, since Ely had already rechecked all of them earlier.

Reassured she wasn't needed, Morgan decided to take a walk up to Wingate to see Jeremy. The exercise would do her aching legs good. Plus, it would give her time to think about everything that had happened with Ely and how her feelings toward him were changing. Well, not exactly changing. She'd always cared for him. But now those feelings had deepened into more. Her step had a bit of extra bounce now.

Trust me, he'd said that day they'd picnicked on the summit with the kids.

The thrilling, terrifying thing she realized now was that she did.

She trusted Ely Malik, against all odds.

The rest of her trek to Wingate passed in a blur. She couldn't say exactly when she'd gone from doubt to certainty where he was concerned. Maybe it was the way Ely showed such kindness for those around him. Of how he always put others first. Or his devotion and loyalty to his family and friends. Ben had had a lot of good qualities, too, at first, she could admit now. But his main focus had always been his career and his status as a surgeon. When they'd married, she'd known that, but she had thought eventually that would change. She'd been wrong. So wrong.

She didn't worry about that with Ely, though. He would remain as he was.

Even to his own detriment.

Morgan stepped up on the granite steps under the portico at Wingate and knocked.

"Come in!" Jeremy opened the door for her with a delighted smile. "Perfect timing. I just finished a fresh batch of croissants for breakfast. We can sit and you can tell me all about your sea rescue last night."

Morgan wasn't even surprised he knew all about it now. She chuckled and followed him to the kitchen, inhaling the delectable scents of pastry dough and butter, then sat on a stool at the island to relay the previous evening's events, interrupted here and there by Jeremy's gasps.

Once she'd finished, he said, "The Malik men are something else, aren't they?"

Seeing as how she'd only met the one, Morgan shrugged. "Well, Ely was pretty amazing last night, that's for sure."

"Were you scared? I'd have been terrified."

Strangely enough, Morgan hadn't been. Not really. There'd been moments when she'd worried about the patients and more than once when she'd been terrified for Ely, but she'd never been truly scared for herself. She shook her head. "This sounds weird, but I honestly loved every minute of it. It reminded me of my time in Africa. And working in the busy ER in Boston. I guess I've grown accustomed to the adrenaline rushes. Last night was oddly exhilarating, actually." She smiled. "And to think I came to the island for the peace and quiet."

Jeremy laughed. "Yeah. How's that working out for you?"

"How's what working out?" Ely stood in the doorway to the kitchen, and Morgan's pulse tumbled.

"Oh, hey, Ely." Jeremy stood, winking at

Morgan. "Come join us. We were discussing your heroics last night."

"Heroics?" He scowled and walked over to the island, touching the bandage on his forehead. "Getting beaned by a low ceiling going downstairs wasn't exactly a superhero moment for me." He stopped next to Morgan, the heat of him brushing her side and making her shiver with delight. He nudged her slightly, smiling down at her. "Luckily, I had the best surgeon on the island stitch me up."

Morgan stared down at the granite-topped island, unexpected euphoria swelling inside her at his compliment. She'd done millions of sutures in her career, could probably do them blindfolded. But Ely's sutures were the most important ones by far to her.

Her voice sounded thick to her own ears as she choked out a thank-you past her constricted vocal cords. Good Lord. She felt like a giddy teenager with her first crush. Morgan glanced up and found the same answering emotions in Ely's tawny gaze. The simmering heat inside her notched higher toward full boil, and despite her realizations about trusting him, this was all feeling too overwhelming. Morgan scrambled off her stool, desperate to get out of there before she tackled Ely to the floor and had her wicked way with him right there in the kitchen. She smoothed a hand down her jeans, palms damp. "I, uh, should get back to the cottage. Thanks for the coffee, Jeremy."

"No problem." He gave her a knowing little smile. "I've had an idea—I thought we could go up to Oak Harbor with Dylan and Gina this morning, since it's Sunday and they're out of school. We'll do some shopping, have lunch. And we still need to get you a costume for the charity ball, too. We can be ready to leave in an hour. What do you think?"

"Uh, that sounds great. Yep." Morgan edged toward the back door, discombobulated. "I'll just go and get ready. See you soon."

Except Ely foiled her escape, following behind her. "I'll come with you. I need to talk to the landscaper about decorations for the ball. Usually Raina handles that, but with her in Paris, it falls to me. Don't want to forget with work and all. We only have three weeks left, right?"

Three weeks.

When Morgan had first arrived here, a month had sounded like forever. Now, it was slipping by so fast. "Yeah," she said quietly, her former happiness dampened. "That's not much time."

"No, it's not." Ely gave her a pointed look

as they walked across the patio together, then he turned to face her, stepping closer. "I don't like to waste time, Morgan. Come sailing with me later this afternoon, after you and Jeremy get back from Oak Harbor. I'll meet you at *The Nightingale* at two."

It wasn't a question. Not that Morgan would've declined. In fact, based on how her pulse was falling all over itself in anticipation, she couldn't wait. Whatever Ely had planned, she'd have the sea, the sun and the man she wanted more than her next breath all to herself. What more could she need?

CHAPTER TEN

AN HOUR LATER, Jeremy, Morgan and the kids clambered into her sedan and started the forty-minute drive up to Oak Harbor at the northern end of the island. Dylan and Gina were excited but trying to be on their best behavior, because ice cream was the reward. And once they were there, true to his word, Jeremy took her to the premier party shop on Whidbey Island to try on costumes. Pirate wench, sexy nurse, courtesan. None looked quite right. Too short, too tight, too revealing.

While she stayed in the dressing room, Jeremy continued to sort through a rack of outfits and every so often pulled one out to pass through the curtains to her. She was beginning to think they'd never find one. Then Jeremy handed in a mermaid costume made of shimmering, silky green material with sequins and an iridescent faux shell–encrusted bodice.

"Oh! I think this one might be it!" he said, glee in his voice. "The color will bring out your blue eyes. Try it on, then let me see!"

Morgan gave the costume a skeptical look. Up close, she could see what had first appeared to be a lot of revealing areas were covered in flesh-toned mesh, so there was that. But the neckline still plunged far lower than she would've liked. She changed into the costume, then checked her reflection in the mirror, turning this way and that to see all angles. Huh. Looked better than she'd imagined. The slinky fabric clung to her body in all the right places without being too tight, and the color did make her eyes pop. Jeremy was right, this was the one. She made a few final adjustments, then pulled aside the dressing room curtain for her friend to see.

Jeremy wolf whistled. "You look ah-mazing! Everyone at the ball will be enchanted." He glanced over at the kids, who were playing in the corner, then leaned in to whisper, "Including Ely."

"Stop it," she said, unable to wipe the grin from her face. They weren't there yet, but maybe this afternoon would change things. She did a little twirl, holding her sparkly green mermaid tail out to the side, enjoying the sensuous feel of the fabric against her skin. Yep. Maybe this afternoon would change a whole lot of things.

"I know where we can get you some shoes," Jeremy said. "And a matching mask."

The kids giggled when Morgan looked over at them, then checked her watch. Almost noon now. Wow. They'd been in there for ages. "Maybe after we get a quick lunch?"

"Good idea."

Morgan went back in the dressing room to change while Jeremy returned to keeping Dylan and Gina occupied. Once she'd paid for her costume rental, they walked to a diner down the block. Halfway there, however, Dylan stopped her by hugging her legs.

"I like you being here, Dr. Salas," the little boy said, beaming up at her. "I hope you never leave."

Morgan's eyes stung, and her answering smile wobbled. "Aw. I like being here with you, too."

She had to clear her throat, her voice rough with affection as she moved them out of the line of traffic on the busy sidewalk.

Jeremy came to her rescue then, sending her a "that's so precious" look. "Come on, kids. Race you to the diner!"

* * *

The morning went by far too slowly for Ely. He ended up going back into the clinic to distract himself, then on a few house calls. Then, finally, it was time to head to the dock.

Honestly, he hadn't looked forward to something this much since Dylan was born. The weather today was what they called heavy—bright and sunny and surprisingly warm, but blustery as hell, making the waves choppy and strong. Challenging conditions for any sailor. Also exhilarating if you knew what you were doing. Steering the fishermen's boat to safety the way she had, Morgan had already proved she could more than handle it.

He checked his smart watch again. Nearly two now. His skin tingled all over as he continued prepping the boat, fingers a bit clumsy as he tied knots and tested ropes. Then she was there, the woman foremost in his thoughts for days—for years, really. Morgan waved as she walked out onto the dock, wearing a pink shirt and denim shorts that showed off her tanned curves to perfection. She waved again and called to him, "Hey."

"Hey," Ely said, straightening, hands on hips, heart in throat. "Ready to go?"

"More than ready." She grinned, then took

his hand to steady her as she climbed aboard. "But I should warn you. You're going to get wet today. Very, very wet, if I have my way."

Her confidence made his body tighten even more. Never one to back down, he gave the cheekiness right back to her. "And you should know us islanders are never worried about getting wet. Besides, if I remember right, didn't we both go under on our last trip?"

She gave him a look, and Ely laughed. She didn't argue. How could she? It was true. But that twinkle in her eye was pure delight. Ely knew better than most how a boat could soar across the sound when it was set to the wind. How shortening the sails with roller reefing genoas and using a smaller jib could increase your speed and your control. How harnessing the power of the wind and battling the waves could be a mind-blowing experience. Almost as good as sex.

Almost.

And speaking of sex, it wasn't his top priority today, believe it or not. Not that he didn't want Morgan. He did. So much it hurt. And his hand was a poor substitute for the real thing. But he also didn't want to rush her. He knew she had scars from her past. He did, too. Today was about spending time together, away from work, talking through those old wounds from the past. Then afterward, if they both wanted it…

Ely swallowed hard and glanced at Morgan again. She looked happy today. Relaxed. Free. Freer than he'd ever seen her since she arrived on the island earlier this month. He took that as a good sign.

CHAPTER ELEVEN

MORGAN, TOO, CHECKED over *The Nightingale* because it kept her from checking out Ely. His outfit was similar to hers—shorts, T-shirt, sneakers. She had a bikini on under her clothes, and he had on board shorts again. He looked good, but then he always did. Ely had a way of making anything he wore flatter his body, all lithe male sinew and strength. Inside, she fizzed with expectation and molten need. Then she glanced up, and their gazes locked.

Oh, boy. Morgan looked away fast, taking far too much interest in the life vest in front of her. Nerve endings alight, she straightened and set the thing aside, concentrating on the trip ahead and not the dryness of her mouth. "I'll take her out this time. I think I remember the channel you followed."

Ely nodded and cast off. As soon as they were in clear water, Morgan set the sails, her confidence growing alongside the thump of blood in her ears. This was it. "I'm helmsman and you're crew. Ready?"

"Ready."

Within seconds they were traveling at speed. The brisk wind caught the sails, and Morgan hooked her feet under the toe strap, easing herself over the side and the rough waves, counterbalancing the cant of the boat with her weight, reveling in the speed. God, she'd missed this. The freedom, the catharsis, the rightness of it all. Morgan pulled the sails in tighter, and the boat went faster still. She shouted to Ely over the roar of the wind, "Dr. Greg said I should take her out and put her through her paces whenever I wanted, so that's what I'm doing."

He joined her at the sail, copying her position then giving a whoop of pure excitement. "Amazing!"

They tacked upwind for the next forty minutes, working as if they'd sailed together for years. Eventually, however, Morgan's muscles protested, and she allowed the boat to bear away from the wind, slowing them to a more sedate pace.

"That was fantastic. Seriously. I've never experienced anything like it," Ely said. "Who taught you how to do that?"

"My dad. He started taking me out when I was four." She smiled. "I've always loved it." She looked over at him, feeling slightly flushed from the adrenaline pounding through her veins. "I even had the chance to join the pre-Olympic training squad but turned it down to study for my MCATs instead."

"Wow." Ely looked impressed. "I've never known anyone else like you, Morgan."

"Same, Ely. Same." She stared at the sparkling waters of Puget Sound, chest squeezing. Ely was such a good man. Not the idealized version she'd kept in her head for years. But genuinely good and true. Whip-smart intelligent, loyal to a fault, sexy as hell, dedicated to those he cared for. If she'd been a person who believed in fate, she might have wondered if it hadn't been love that had drawn her back here again after all these years.

The realization brought her up short.

Love? She didn't love Ely.

Do I?

She definitely liked him. A lot. More than a lot. It had nothing to do with his money or his name or even his looks. It had to do with how kind he was, how he knew the right thing to say at the right time to make people feel better. The way her heart raced and her knees went tingly whenever he was around. About how she felt comfortable with him, even when they talked about uncomfortable things. About how she missed him when he wasn't there.

Oh, God. I love Ely Malik.

But she was still afraid, too. Afraid of putting herself in that same vulnerable position again that she had with Ben. Afraid of being open and raw, then having that used against her. Anxiety pressed hard on her temples, and Morgan turned back to fiddle with the rigging, wondering when the temperature had risen so much. The last of the clouds had disappeared from the sky, and there were blue skies for miles. They were floating in a secluded little cove off one of the smaller, uninhabited islands. The sun beat down, prickling hot on her skin. She tugged off her T-shirt, revealing her pink bikini top as her shoulders baked.

Ely watched her, silent and still. Then he removed his shirt, too, giving her an eyeful of tanned torso. Her throat tightened as she gazed at all that bronzed skin begging for her touch. His aviator shades again hid his tawny gaze from her, reflecting back her own wanton expression. Her heart tripped as she imagined those brawny arms around her, pressing her against him, hot skin to hot skin, the fullness of his body inside hers, thrusting again and again and…

"How about a swim?" Ely said, his voice tauter than normal as he pointed. "To the beach there. It's not too far."

Morgan nodded, not trusting her words, as Ely dropped anchor. She slipped off her shorts and toed off her sneakers, then stood on the wooden deck at the back of the boat, poised to dive, hoping the exercise would restore her equilibrium.

Then she plunged into the depths, gasping as cold water enveloped her, icy and invigorating as she struck out for shore, not needing to look back to know Ely followed her. It was almost animalistic now, their connection, predator and prey. Though it was anyone's guess which was which. Morgan had nearly reached the shore when a hand tugged on her ankle. She stopped and treaded water as Ely surfaced not far away.

"You didn't wait for me," he said.

"I knew you'd catch up."

You always catch up.

Then he set off again with long, sure strokes, leaving her in his wake and beating her to shore.

"Hey, you cheated," she yelled once she

reached the shallows near the remote pebbled beach. "Competitive much?"

He grinned wide from the beach where he let the waterproof tote on his back fall to the ground at his feet, then opened it to spread out the blanket inside. "Always. You know that, Morgan."

Yep. She did. Another area where they were well matched. To prove it, she splashed water at him. She wouldn't surrender without a fight. Battle lines drawn, Ely slowly faced her, water dripping from his handsome face, then he charged back into the water, sending a small wall of water in her direction. Soon they were play-tussling in the waist-high shallows. He was bigger and taller than her, but she could move more quickly, making it even. At least until he grabbed her by the waist and hoisted her in the air.

"Hey! No fair. What the—?" Morgan yelled, scowling down at him.

Ely held her aloft a moment, and their gazes locked. His eyes darkened, and slowly, so slowly, she slid down his front until they were face-to-face. Her feet still didn't touch bottom, so she wrapped her legs around his waist against the current, and she kissed him. Like she'd been dying to do ever since that night at her cottage. Her heart slammed against her rib cage, desperate for release. His body responded in kind despite the chilly water, his length hardening against her, pulsing with undeniable need.

He carried her back to shore, and they somehow ended up on the blanket without breaking their kiss. She couldn't get enough of him—the way he tasted, the way he smelled, the way he shuddered against her when she stroked the sensitive spot between his shoulder blades. His hands seemed to be everywhere at once—her back, her butt, her breasts, between her legs. Shocks of pleasure zinged through her bloodstream, making her moan low and deep. Ely nuzzled her neck, then made quick work of her bikini top before taking a chilled nipple into his warm, wet mouth. The contrast made Morgan gasp and arch beneath him, crying out softly. It had been so long since she'd felt this alive. Too long.

He continued lavishing attention on her breasts with his lips and tongue as his hands drifted southward, his thumbs tracing under the top of her bikini bottoms, teasing her, making her shiver with need.

More, more, more.

She panted, writhed. "Please, Ely…"

"Please what, *janaan*?" he asked, lifting his head to meet her gaze.

She'd called her that before, at the cottage. Bewildered and bewitched, she focused enough to ask, "What does that mean?"

He blinked at her, eyes glassy with desire, color dotting his high cheekbones and his hard length pulsing against her thigh. Ely frowned, the muscles in his throat working as he swallowed hard. "It's Urdu. My father's family was from Pakistan."

Not an answer, really, but she didn't care anymore because Ely was kissing the skin above her bikini bottoms now, removing them to make love to her where she needed him most. Using his lips and tongue and fingers in the most extraordinary ways to make her feel the most extraordinary things until she cried out in ecstasy so many times that she lost count. By then, Morgan felt light as a feather and heavy as stone all at once. She wanted more, though. So much more. She wanted him, inside her.

She reached for him, only to have Ely stop her, kissing her palm.

"I don't have protection," he whispered against her skin.

"It's all right." She pulled him up for another kiss, tasting herself on his lips. "I can't get pregnant."

He stilled a moment, watching her closer. "Morgan, I…"

But she didn't want to talk about that now. There'd be time later for old hurts and pain. Right now, she just wanted to feel good, to feel free, with Ely. To help him along, she took advantage of his stunned silence to reach down again and stroke him through the soft fabric of his board shorts. Soon, he groaned low and closed his eyes.

"Please, Ely. I need you," she said again, nibbling his jaw.

Cursing under his breath in a language she didn't understand, Ely pulled away to remove his shorts, revealing the full extent of his desire. Then he was beside her again, and Morgan felt aflame from the inside out. She rocked against him, urging him on, scoring her nails lightly down his back as he rose above her, holding his weight on his elbows. Gazes locked, she parted her thighs to allow him easy entry, and he thrust deep inside her, then held still, their bodies joined. When he finally moved, she moved with him, setting a rhythm that had them both teetering on the brink all too soon. It was too much. It would never be enough. Ely reached between them to stroke her slick folds, and Morgan spiraled over the edge to another orgasm, reaching, straining, soaring.

Ely continued to thrust, riding out her pleasure, once, twice, then joining her in orgasm. Waves crashed over them in time to those on the shore, mirroring their sensations until, at last, they floated back to earth. Arms around each other, breaths ragged. Slowly, reality returned. Sunshine. Seagulls cawing in the distance. Pebbles *cushing* beneath their blanket as Ely rolled off her, then pulled her into his side, her head resting over his heart. Sated and happy, Morgan didn't want to break the spell.

At last, Ely said softly, quietly, his fingers tracing lazily up and down her spine, "Why can't you get pregnant?"

Morgan reminded herself to breathe. Even after all this time, it was so hard to talk about it. But it was time. He needed to know, deserved to know. She shifted slightly in his arms, cleared her throat, ignored the swell of grief inside her, then exhaled slow. "About a year and half before Ben died, I got pregnant. Turned out to be ectopic. They operated to remove the embryo lodged in my Fallopian tube and discovered the other one was badly damaged, too, most likely due to endometriosis. The doctors told me kids weren't an option for me. Not biological ones, anyway."

Chest aching and eyes sticky, she stayed where she was, awaiting his reaction, hoping for the best, fearing the worst. Family was so important to Ely. He had Dylan, but if he married again, Ely would want more children, she was sure. He should have more children. He deserved more children, but she couldn't give him that. The realization broke her heart. She continued when he didn't respond, turning her face more into his chest so he couldn't see her tears. "Ben and I… didn't deal with it well. It's one of the things that ultimately drove us apart. I withdrew, and he looked elsewhere for what he needed. For a long time, I felt like it was my fault. Sometimes, I still do…" Then there was no more holding back her grief. She cried, long, wracking sobs that tore at her soul, releasing the pent-up pain and guilt she'd carried for years. Ely held her closer, his face buried in her hair, whispering soothing nothings, letting her get it out of her system.

When she finally settled against him once more, drained to dregs, he whispered, "Jesus, Morgan. I'm so sorry."

She sniffled and held him tighter. "Thank you."

Long moments passed as more memories washed over her. She'd opened the floodgates and now there was no shutting them, apparently. "I was devastated. Ben and I both were. He'd always wanted a big family. At the time, he said it didn't matter, but I knew it did. We pulled away from each other. I threw myself into my work so I didn't have to think about it, so I didn't have to feel. We drifted apart..." Her breath caught on a hiccup. "During the last year of our marriage, we barely spent any time together at all. We ended up like strangers. That's when he started having his affair. Looking back, I guess I can't blame him now. Stuck in a loveless marriage."

Her body tensed as old emotions flared. Regret. Anger. Resentment. Denial. Coming home to an empty house, leaving before Ben was up in the morning. They'd tried at first to fix the broken parts, but after a while it seemed pointless. Too wrapped up in their own pain and loss to notice anything else.

"Then, I got the call one day from the state police." She went numb, frozen, same as when they'd told her Ben was gone. "He'd swerved to miss a car coming the wrong way down the road. Died instantly. I already told you that his mistress was with him. A colleague, going to the same conference." The next words cut like a knife. "She came to see me after the funeral, told me she and Ben had been in love and he hadn't known how to tell me." Morgan shook her head. "I would've given him a divorce. We weren't in love anymore, and I wanted him to be happy."

She sniffled, those last words hanging in the air a long moment before she mumbled, "Sorry."

Ely finally propped up on an elbow to frown down at her. "You have nothing to be sorry about, Morgan. None of that was your fault. Ever." He sat up and pulled her close into a bear hug. "Please stop thinking that way. People do what they do. We're all responsible for our own choices."

They sat there like that for a while then, him holding her, rocking back and forth slowly.

Morgan took a deep breath, somehow lighter, freer, emptier for having released all that. "Thank you for listening, Ely. For being there for me. I came to this island for a chance to start over, and it feels like maybe I have."

"Hmm." He kissed her temple, wrapping the blanket around them, then staring out at the horizon with her back pressed to his front, his legs caging hers in, both still naked. "As I mentioned earlier, my father was from Pakistan," he said, tone low, intimate. Morgan stilled, not wanting to interrupt him, knowing this was important. "My mother was Scottish. They were a great pair. Their talents complemented each other. I loved them very much. My father built his tech company from the ground up. A true American success story. The only time I think he was ever disappointed in me was when I told him I wanted to be a doctor instead of following in his footsteps. Thank God Sam was interested in carrying on the family legacy. My father never held it against me, though. I always knew how proud he was of me. Of both of us. My mother, too."

He smiled against her cheek. "I never really paid much attention to the fact that they were famous growing up. It was just a thing about our lives, like the money my father made. I mean, I knew we were different than a lot of people, but living here on the island, no one gave us special treatment. I had a great childhood, running through the farm fields, getting dirty and muddy, sailing on Puget Sound." His fond smile faltered then. "Then the plane crash happened when I was eighteen. Everything changed in an instant. I had to grow up fast—as the older brother, I had to become caretaker of the estate, the family.

Sam was only ten at the time. He couldn't do it. I had to protect him from all the tabloids and the photographers that descended like vultures. The investigation into their deaths came back as accidental. They'd been flying over the Rockies, and the weather turned bad. Nothing the pilot could do, but that didn't stop people from speculating, from nosing into our private business, from spreading rumors and conspiracy theories."

"Oh, Ely." She placed her hands over his forearms around her middle and squeezed tight. "I'm so sorry."

He nodded, his stubble tickling the side of her neck as he rested his chin on her shoulder. "Me, too. But that's why I'm so protective of those I care for, why I stayed here on the island to raise Dylan, far away from all that." He tightened his hold around her. "It's not a life for everyone, though. It wasn't enough for Raina. I understand if it's not enough for you, either."

Morgan opened her mouth to answer, then stopped herself. They were still lost in the afterglow, still dizzy on sex hormones and requited lust. She knew how she felt, but not Ely. When she made a choice about her future, she wanted to do it with a clear head and a wide-open heart. No regrets, not anymore.

So, instead of answering his unspoken question, she pulled away to kiss him fast then pull on her bikini top. They'd talk again once they got back to the cottage. They had time. No need to rush.

"Today was wonderful, Ely. Thank you." She smiled, tugging on her bikini bottoms, too. "Should we get back to the boat?"

"I guess we should," he said at last, standing to tug on his board shorts, averting his gaze. They swam back to the boat, raised anchor and set sail for home. The wind had picked up enough again to use the sails, and the late-afternoon sunshine was still warm. Morgan kept trying to touch him or catch his eye to make him smile, but he seemed to be putting some distance between them.

"Everything okay?" she asked at one point, concerned.

"Fine." He smiled, but his eyes were hidden behind his sunglasses again, so she couldn't tell what he was really thinking.

As they approached the bay, Morgan saw a figure standing outside the cottage, eyes shielded, looking out over the water. Jeremy. From the way he was pacing back and forth, he was agitated. She tensed. Something must be wrong. Was it Gina again?

Ely must've noticed at the same time she

did, because he hurried to pull on his T-shirt and shoved his feet into his shoes before starting to take down the sails. "Something's up."

They reached the dock, and Ely hopped over the side to tie up the boat, then headed to the cottage without waiting for Morgan. As she finished sorting everything out on the boat, she kept an eye on Jeremy and Ely in the distance. Next thing she knew, Ely climbed into his truck and took off. Her anxiety notched higher. So much for talking about the future. It would have to wait until later.

By the time she hurried up the hill to the cottage where Jeremy still waited, her gut was in knots. "What's going on?"

"It's Dylan. I wasn't too worried at first, because I figured he'd probably caught the same bug Gina had earlier. Then the pain in his stomach got worse and… Oh, God." His words rushed out in a torrent of nervous frustration. "I tried to get ahold of Ely, but his phone was out of range, then I tried the clinic in Langley but couldn't get them, either. Then I rushed over here, and luckily you guys were coming in."

"Okay. It's okay, Jeremy." Morgan patted his shoulder, switching into full-on doctor mode now. "You did the right thing. Let me change, then we'll go back to Wingate to-gether, all right?"

She darted inside, tugging off her bikini and T-shirt, exchanging them for jeans and a clean Harvard sweatshirt, then she scooped up her medical kit and hurried back outside to where Jeremy stood near her sedan. "Try not to worry, okay? Kids are tougher than they look."

Ten minutes later, they hurried through the grand foyer of Wingate and up to Dylan's room.

Ely was there already, examining his son, worry etched on his face. He glanced up at Morgan, frowning. "I'm almost certain it's appendicitis." He pressed gently on the boy's lower right abdomen, then released. Dylan moaned and squirmed in pain. "Positive for guarding as well."

"I want Mommy," Dylan cried, and Mor-gan's heart clenched. "Where's Mommy?"

"She's working, remember?" Ely crouched beside the bed to smooth damp hair from Dylan's forehead. "I'll call her. Promise. Right now, though, I need you to let Daddy finish examining you, okay?"

He looked up Morgan, eyes filled with an-guish, and she placed a supportive hand on Ely's shoulder. A burst appendix was nothing to mess around with. Left untreated, it could lead to sepsis or worse.

"How about if I take a look instead?" she asked quietly. There was a reason you didn't treat your family members—loss of objectivity could often lead to bad decisions.

A beat or two passed before Ely gave a curt nod and moved aside. Morgan stepped in to perform the same exam and reached the same conclusion. "It's definitely appendicitis. What do you want to do?"

"Remove it." Ely raked a hand through his tousled hair. There was still sand on his feet. On her feet, too. Her chest felt heavy and tight. The surgery was relatively common nowadays, but that didn't make his decision any easier. Morgan wished she could comfort him, but now wasn't the time or place.

"Should we airlift him to Seattle General?" she asked.

"No," Ely said. "I'm afraid there isn't time."

"We'll do it at the clinic, then. I'll scrub in." Morgan had done her fair share of appendectomies, too. "Can Dr. Lake do the anesthesia again?"

Ely looked at her, pulling on his ear. "Are you sure you can handle this?"

It wasn't personal, his doubt. She knew that. It was the normal concern of a parent for a child, intensified because of what Ely had been through growing up. Her rational mind knew that. But it didn't stop the pinch of hurt inside her. Morgan tamped it down as best she could and gave him a firm nod. Time to put the personal aside in favor of the professional. Something she'd become all too adept at lately. "I am. I did many of these during my mission trip in Africa. But if you'd feel more comfortable calling in another surgeon from Langley, then that's what we'll do."

He blew out his cheeks, pinching the bridge of his nose, eyes closed. "I just want the best for him."

"I know." She squared her shoulders, determined to put Ely's fears at ease as she would with any other patient's father. "I'm confident I can handle Dylan's surgery." The boy cried out again, then writhed on the bed, flushed and in agony. "But whatever you decide, you need to hurry. The longer we wait, the higher the risk of rupture."

Ely cursed and stared down at his son, then looked back up at her. "Let's call the air ambulance first. Get a rough estimate of their ETA. We can also prep the surgery room at the clinic. That way if things go south before they arrive, then you can step in."

"Good." She crouched by the bedside again,

reaching over to stroke the boy's fevered brow. "Dylan, you need an operation on your tummy. You won't feel anything because you'll be asleep, okay? We're going to move you now to get you to the hospital. Understand?"

"Will Daddy do it?" he asked, his tone plaintive.

"No, buddy," Ely said, taking his son's hand and moving in beside Morgan. "But I'll be right beside you the whole time, and I'll be there when you wake up, too. Promise."

"What about Mommy?" Tears filled Dylan's eyes.

"I promise you I'll call her and let her know what's going on." Ely's Adam's apple bobbed. "She'll be there as soon as she can. She loves you very much. You know that, right?"

Dylan nodded, and Ely gently hugged his son, whispering something to him, and Dylan finally relaxed in his father's embrace. Morgan realized then that it wasn't just Ely she loved. It was Dylan, too. She'd do everything in her power to make sure the little boy made a full recovery.

"Morgan, get ahold of Sandy and have her call Seattle General, please," Ely said as he carried his son to the door. "I'll drive him to the clinic in my truck. He can lie down on the seat in the back. And tell Sandy to call

Dr. Lake, too, before she goes in to get the surgery room set up."

"Done," Morgan said, following him downstairs. "It's going to be all right."

Ely gave her a side glance, looking unconvinced.

"Jeremy," he called to his chef in the foyer. "Call Raina. Let her know I'll update her when I can. And call Sam, too. You have his number."

By the time they reached the clinic, Dylan's condition had worsened. Ely hurried inside with his son in his arms. Morgan met him at the door and filled him in on Sandy's conversations with the hospital on the mainland.

"Seattle General will send the air ambulance, but there was an accident on the I-5 and they're tied up triaging that. They'll work us in, but it could be up to an hour before they get here. We also need to factor in the travel time back to the hospital." Dylan moaned loudly, and Morgan leveled Ely with a pointed stare, "My professional opinion is we shouldn't wait."

He held his son a little bit tighter, the most precious thing in his world, as if that could keep him safe. As if that could make him well. *Dammit*. He shouldn't have gone out sailing with Morgan. If he'd been home at Wingate, maybe he could have caught this sooner, given them more time, more options for Dylan's treatment. Less risk. More control. That was what happened when he took his eye off the ball.

He should have known better.

Morgan took a deep breath, her tone calm and patient. "As you know, Ely, the longer we wait, the more likely Dylan is to have complications. It should be a straightforward procedure. If it's done now."

"Dr. Lake's on the way," Sandy called down the hall where they stood. "Be here in twenty."

Ely stared at Morgan. An hour ago, they'd been cuddling on the beach, happy and carefree. Not this.

It wasn't enough for Raina. I understand if it's not enough for you, either...

He wanted Morgan to stay. Wanted to make a life with her, but not if she didn't want that, too.

He'd been there, done that, trying to make someone stay, trying to make it work when it wouldn't. He couldn't go back to that again. He couldn't let this interfere with his son's treatment. Morgan had switched back to professional mode here, and he needed to do the same. His feelings didn't matter.

What mattered was Dylan and making him better.

"Fine. We'll do it here." Ely's mouth pressed into a grim line. "But I'm scrubbing in, too."

For a moment, Morgan looked like she wanted to argue, but she didn't. "Okay. But only to observe."

CHAPTER TWELVE

ELY DID OBSERVE. Morgan felt his gaze on her the entire time—not intimidating, per se, but stressful. With Dr. Lake manning the anesthesia and Sandy acting as her surgical nurse, Morgan made her first small incision, then another, working precisely and methodically until Dylan's inflamed appendix was exposed.

"Irrigation, please." She waited as Sandy cleared the area with sterile saline.

From there it was as textbook perfect a surgery as she could have hoped for. A few snips, a pair of clamps to tie off the blood vessels and then she was placing the removed tissue into a specimen tray to send to the lab. Normally this procedure was done laparoscopically, but the clinic didn't have that equipment, so she'd done it the old-fashioned way.

Immediate danger over now, Morgan exhaled behind her mask, then began closing. Based on the size and inflammation of that appendix, they'd made the right choice to do the surgery now. It would've ruptured before the air ambulance arrived.

Dylan should make a full and swift recovery. With a small scar as a memento.

Ely remained by his son's side as Morgan stepped back from the operating table, relief and gratitude shining in his eyes over the top of his mask.

After Dr. Lake finished with the anesthesia, they wheeled Dylan into a small recovery area set up next door. The kid was coming around already, but it would still be several hours before he was fully conscious again. He'd probably need a couple of days in the hospital in Seattle, too, to recuperate.

Sandy caught Ely as he followed Morgan into the scrub room. "Dylan's mother is on hold. I brought her up to speed, but she still wants to talk to you."

"I'll be right there." Once the door closed behind Sandy, Ely turned to Morgan, his voice gruff. "Thank you. You did an excellent job."

"You're welcome." She blinked back sudden tears, wanting to hug him, but not daring to in front of all the staff. "I'm glad it all worked out."

They stood there watching each other until Ely backed toward the door. "I need to take that call."

Morgan finished cleaning up, then went next door to the recovery area to check on her patient. Ely was there already at Dylan's bedside, cell phone to his ear. She started to back out quietly to give them some privacy, but not before hearing a bit of their conversation.

"Daddy?" Dylan said, his voice rough from the anesthetic. "Am I fixed?"

"You are. A few days of rest and you'll be all better." Ely bent and kissed his son's forehead, then stroked his hair. The sweetness of it all made her heart ache in the best way. He was such a good father—caring, attentive, engaged. She knew how much being there meant to Ely. She might not be able to have children of her own, but she'd love and care for Dylan like he was her very own. If Ely wanted that, too. She didn't want to get too far ahead of herself, though. They still needed to talk.

Ely spoke into the phone, then turned back to his son. "Mommy says she's flying back from Paris early to be with you. She'll be here before you know it."

She must've made a noise, because Ely

and Dylan both looked over at her. Morgan winced slightly. "Sorry. Didn't mean to interrupt."

"Come in," Ely said, waving her over. "Dylan was asking about you."

"You were?" she asked, stepping up to the boy's bedside.

"Will you stay with me until Mommy gets here?" Dylan looked far too small in the big bed. "Please?"

Morgan glanced from him to Ely, who was watching her closely, then propped her hip on the opposite side of the bed from Ely. In the back of her mind, a warning bell sounded. She was getting too far ahead of herself, getting too attached, too soon, but she couldn't just walk away. Not now. Not yet. She took Dylan's hand and smiled, eyes stinging again. "I'll stay as long as you two need me," she promised, meaning every word. "Now, try and get some sleep."

The next few days Ely didn't see much of Morgan, unfortunately. When he wasn't working at the clinic, he spent his spare time at Seattle General with Dylan. Raina had kept her word and taken a red-eye flight back from Paris and was there, too, rearranging her schedule during her son's recovery.

In the quiet moments alone, though, Ely's mind returned to the beach with Morgan. Honestly, being with her, holding her afterward, had been some of the best moments in his life—at least until she'd not answered him. He was a cautious man by nature, and he'd known from the start she was leaving at the end of the month, so part of him knew he shouldn't be bothered now. He'd gone into this knowing it was temporary. Knowing you couldn't force someone to do something they didn't want. That never worked out well in the end. And while the sex between them had been amazing, it was more than just the physical attraction for him. Always had been. Even if Morgan would never feel the same.

Looking back, he could see he'd fallen for her so hard, so deep, so fast it felt like a whirlwind. Which only served to trigger his already buzzing control issues. Ely was trying to do better with this stuff, but it was difficult. And the last thing he wanted to do was make Morgan think she had to stay here out of some sense of loyalty to him or their past. He certainly didn't want to put his son through another messy breakup. Couldn't put himself through that, either, if he was honest. Being vulnerable only to lose her in the end.

Then again, he feared it was already too late for him with Morgan.

The last car ferry of the day docked at Clinton, and Ely drove onto dry land, deciding to stop at the cottage and see if she was home. This was silly, speculating and guessing when they should just sit down and talk it out. It was after eleven now, a bit late, but hopefully she'd still be up.

The lights were on in the cottage when he pulled to a stop in her drive, and now he was second-guessing himself. Maybe he should go home and get a good night's sleep. Come back in the morning when he was clearheaded. But no. He couldn't do that. They both had to work the next day. There never seemed to be enough time to talk about things. Why wasn't there enough time?

His gut tensed. It wasn't nerves, really. Just uncertainty. Ely liked to know what he was walking into, and he had no clue with Morgan. It brought up unpleasant memories of the time after his parents had died, when everything had been so chaotic and scary and sad. He'd had to step up and be the man of the house then, even though he'd felt very much not ready. Sam had needed him. Same as Dylan needed him now. He was used to putting others' needs ahead of his own for the sake of the greater good. But now it was just him and Morgan, and he needed to know.

So, he took a deep breath, then got out of the truck and walked up to knock on the door.

Morgan opened it, looking far too adorable in her pink flannel pj's and socks. His heart rate kicked up another notch. "Uh, hi."

"Hi," she said, giving him a curious look. "I wasn't expecting you tonight. Come in."

She moved aside to let him enter, and as he passed by, Ely caught the scent of her flowery shampoo, taking him right back to the beach, to making love on that blanket, her warm, welcoming body tight and wet around him, and...

Stop that.

His throat constricted, and his heart thumped harder. He was here to talk, that was all. Given how tired he was, he wasn't up for anything else, anyway. He followed her over to the sofa and sat down, lifting his arm over her shoulders when she cuddled against him, warm and soft.

This was nice. Cozy. He could get used to this. That was the problem.

They shared a brief kiss, then she tucked her head under his chin. It felt good. Too good. He was never going to get through this if he let his emotions get the better of him.

Distance. He needed to keep some distance. Distance and control. "How was your afternoon?"

"Fine," she said, her body relaxed against his. "Yours? How's Dylan doing?"

"Much better. I was just on my way home, actually, and thought I'd stop by."

"I'm glad you did."

A fire crackled cheerfully in the fireplace, and a mug of cocoa and an open book, spine up, sat on the coffee table. But the air smelled of wood smoke and desperation. Morgan had her arms around his waist, and her head rested on his chest over his heart. Which was aching and pounding, all at the same time.

Just ask her. Out with it...

As if hearing his thoughts, Morgan leaned up to look at him. "Something particular on your mind?"

"Uh…" An odd mix of arousal and apprehension zipped through his bloodstream. Why couldn't he just say what he wanted? Yes, it was scary, but he'd been scared before and pushed on. Maybe he was getting sidetracked by his body's response to her, which only intensified his anxiety at his lack of control. He scooted away from her, dropping his arm to his side, frowning. "How do you feel about things? Between us, I mean."

Smooth. Not.

Morgan tilted her head a little, her expression thoughtful. "Good, I think. Why?"

"Oh, well. I just wondered…"

Why didn't you say anything that day on the beach? Do you not want to be with me?

He scowled down at his hands in his lap, then fiddled with the buttons on his shirt. Being direct wasn't so easy when your heart was involved, so he asked a more roundabout question. "Have you thought about staying on at the clinic after Dr. Greg gets back?"

Morgan's brows drew together. "Um. I didn't know that was even an option."

Hell. What a stupid thing to ask, especially since she was right. He and Dr. Greg had never discussed taking on a permanent third partner. God, he was making a mess of all this. "Forget it. Not sure why I asked that. I'm sure you're more than ready to go when your time is up here, right? Probably already have some big job lined up back on the mainland and everything."

She blinked slowly, a bit of the old wariness slipping back into her expression. She bit her lip and went still, looking away. "Actually, I have been thinking a lot about my future lately."

"Oh?" He glanced up at her again.

Morgan nodded, scooting back to the far corner of the sofa. She was obviously skittish. He couldn't blame her.

Ely stood to walk over the fireplace, needing to move, needing to expel some of his nervous energy before it ate him alive. He'd made a mess of this whole thing. Of course, it didn't help knowing more about Morgan's past and trying to walk through that minefield, but still. He should've waited. Even as the clock ticked down on what little time they had together.

"Sorry," he said, scrubbing a hand over his face then staring down at the flames, the searing heat doing nothing to chase away the chill inside him. "Seeing Dylan on that operating table, then later in recovery crying for his mother and her not being there…"

He swore under his breath. "My main goal over the years has been stability. I've done my absolute best to create a stable life for myself and my son here on the island. Then you came along and blew that all to pieces. And while I've loved every minute of it, and while I—" He almost let the words slip out, but stopped himself. Ely hung his head and squeezed his eyes shut. "I shouldn't have said what I did on the beach. Pressuring you about seeing yourself living here on the island. That was a mistake. I never should've asked that. I'm sorry."

"I see," she replied, but from her tight tone, Ely doubted she did.

"Do you?"

She grabbed a throw pillow and hugged it tight against her like a shield. "We all say things we don't mean sometimes. Believe me, no one knows that better than me."

Ouch.

Okay, yes. This was definitely going off the rails.

Abort! Abort!

Stupid Ely. Always trying to do too many things at once. Always trying to control everything. God, he was so bad at this. He rubbed the back of his neck, wishing for a complete reset of this conversation, yet knowing it was already too late for that. "I, uh, I should get home. Early day tomorrow."

"Hmm." Her voice cracked slightly, letting him know she wasn't as okay as she pretended. Every fiber of his being wanted to go to her, to kneel and beg her to stay, but he didn't, because that would only make this whole situation even more pathetic.

So, he headed for the door instead. Stopped on the threshold, staring down at his shaking hand on the knob, looked back at her one last time. "Three weeks left."

Morgan didn't get up, just watched him from the sofa, her smile bleak. "Yes. Three weeks left."

Those three little words—not the three little words he'd wanted to say—sucker punched him in the gut. They continued to pummel him all the way back to his truck. This was exactly why he usually kept to himself. Why he didn't open his heart to anyone. Why he didn't take risks. Because in the end, they always came back to hurt you.

CHAPTER THIRTEEN

THE REST OF the month passed by in a blur for Morgan. Between work and home and back again, she lost track of the days. She and Ely barely spoke now, other than passing pleasantries at the clinic, and it reminded her far too much of the final days of her marriage to Ben. A half-life of grays and beiges with no bright colors at all. Funny how things changed so fast. Things had been so good between them that day on the beach, until they weren't anymore.

She'd allowed him in, past her barriers. She'd trusted him. And look where it had gotten her.

Right back where she'd started.

Well, no more. She was done trusting people.

By the time the day of the costume ball arrived, Morgan didn't want to go anymore, but Dr. Greg and Peggy were arriving back from

Australia, and they'd expect her to be there. So, she forced herself to get up and face Halloween, refusing to give in to the hurt inside her. She'd survived worse. She'd get through this, too. Eventually.

It would help once she was off the island, away from Ely. Seeing him every day, working with him, knowing they wouldn't be together, had been almost unbearable. But she'd worked hard to put on a happy facade, pretending everything was okay, keeping things light and normal in front of everyone else, as if her heart hadn't been ripped out and stomped on. She'd only been here a month, only been reunited with Ely for a few weeks, and yet she'd loved him. And she'd lost him, and deep inside she feared this might be it—the thing that broke her once and for all.

She absently tapped her spoon against the shell of the soft-boiled egg she'd made for breakfast to crack it, but as soon as the sunny yellow yolk ran out, a sudden wave of nausea washed over her, and she barely made it to the bathroom in time. Afterward, she sat on the tile floor, hot face pressed to the cool porcelain of the toilet, waiting for her heaving stomach to settle. Maybe she was coming down with something? On the bright side, that could be a genuine reason not to go to the ball tonight.

"Knock, knock. Is there a doctor in the house?" Jeremy let himself in, then walked into the bedroom, halting at the sight of Morgan on the bathroom floor. "Good Lord, what happened to you?"

He helped her up and placed a cool washcloth on back of her neck, then stood nearby as she sat on the edge of the bed, apparently concerned she might faint or something.

Morgan took a few deep breaths, then looked up at him. "I think I'm coming down with something."

"Oh, no! Don't say that. You can't miss the ball tonight. Everyone will be there." Jeremy smiled. "Including Sam."

The last thing in the world she wanted to do at that moment was meet more Maliks. She sat up, glad some of her dizziness was subsiding, and forced a smile for her friend. "I feel like I know him already, since you've said such nice things about him. How are things with you two now that he's back at Wingate?"

"Good." Jeremy blushed and took a seat beside her. He had it bad, that much was obvious. "Always nice to reconnect whenever he's here to visit." His besotted grin beamed brighter than the sun, casting her own heartache in deeper shadows. "Sam's so charming and nice and wonderful." Then his smile faded, and his shoulders slumped. "But I'm not sure he's as enamored with me. I mean, I'm just the chef. And I've got Gina." Jeremy shook his head. "It could all be a one-sided crush on my part, but I can't help myself."

She put her arm around his shoulders. "You are not just the chef, Jeremy. You're a funny, smart, talented man raising a child all on his own. And you're an excellent cook. Sam would be lucky to have you. Any man would be lucky to have you."

Jeremy laughed, then hugged her, and Morgan felt slightly better. If nothing else came from her stay on Whidbey Island, she'd made a good friend in him. But she was leaving Sunday night, the day after the ball, and that made her sad. There was no way she could stay, though, not without a job and with constant reminders of Ely around every corner. She'd thought she'd hidden her misery pretty well, but apparently not, because Jeremy gave her a speculative stare.

"What's wrong?"

Morgan shook her head. "Nothing. Just thinking about everything I have to do once I leave."

"Liar." He nudged her with his shoulder.

"Dr. Greg might offer you a permanent spot at the clinic."

"No, he won't." Morgan sighed. Ely had said as much during their last ill-fated conversation. "Besides, I promised my parents I'd visit them next month." Not the whole truth, but not a total lie, either. She really did have those things to do, even if the real reason she couldn't stay was Ely.

"But I thought you loved it here. And you seemed so happy. Is it too boring? It is, isn't it?"

"Uh, no." Morgan chuckled. "My time here has been anything but boring."

"I'll miss you. I hope you'll stay in touch."

"Or course I will."

Morgan stared at her hands in her lap for fear Jeremy would see the tears in her eyes. God, she'd been so emotional lately, too, above and beyond the regular breakup-heartache stuff. What was even happening to her?

"Dylan will miss you, too. And Gina. And Ely." He reached over and covered her hands with his. "You know, Ely has this weird way of thinking that putting his family first means putting himself last, but that's not true. The best thing he can do for Dylan is to show him what a healthy, loving relationship looks like. I love Ely like a brother and want to see him happy. He needs someone to share his life with, someone who shares his passions and interests, someone who cares for him as much as he deserves. Someone like you, Morgan."

It took a second for her brain to register his words. She looked up at him, startled. "What?"

"You heard me." Jeremy gave her a look. "I can see you love him. It's been written all over your face since a week after you got here. Remind me to play poker with you. You're a horrible bluff."

Oh, God.

She felt sick again, for totally different reasons now. She couldn't live through all the pitying looks again, not after what she went through with Ben. "Please don't tell anyone, Jeremy. I'll get over it. I have to, since he doesn't love me back."

Jeremy snorted. "If that's true, then Ely's a bigger idiot than I thought in this situation. You two are perfect for each other. And he cares for you. I know he does, because he gets that sappy look on his face whenever he sees you. If he said otherwise, it's probably just to protect himself."

Morgan took that in. Ely hadn't really ever said one way or another whether he loved her. She'd just assumed based on his actions the past few weeks that he didn't. But maybe that wasn't fair. He'd had a lot on his plate to deal with, so...

"Look. He sees it as his duty to look out for everyone. So, he works hard to stay in control. My guess is, you're a risk to all that."

"But I'd never do anything to hurt him or Dylan."

"Yes, but if Ely feels things are out of his hands—the way emotions usually are—then he withdraws. It's all about protection with him, remember?"

Jeremy stood then and sighed. "Well, I better get back to Wingate. I've got a ton to get done before the ball tonight. Keeping an eye on the caterers, and God forbid everything's not perfect when Mrs. MacIntosh takes over for me later." He stopped at the door and looked back at her over his shoulder. "Pick you up at six thirty?"

Morgan nodded, still distracted by what he'd told her. Was it possible she'd been wrong these past few weeks? After he left, she cleaned up her now-cold breakfast, her thoughts tumbling like wet socks in a dryer. It wasn't even noon yet. She should do something. Take a walk. Get outside. Then she caught a glimpse of herself in the mirror, and *ugh*. She looked like hell—face pale, dark circles under her eyes. She hadn't been sleeping well, either, come to think of it. Though that wasn't surprising under the circumstances. Partway through changing her clothes, another wave of nausea hit, and she ran to the bathroom again.

Man, she hadn't been sick to her stomach like this since…

She sat back on her heels, bile burning her throat and breath ragged.

No. No, no, no.

Her butt hit the bathroom floor, and she held on to the toilet for dear life. It wasn't possible. It couldn't be possible. Her period was late, sure, but that could be from stress. And the doctors had told her the chances of her conceiving again were slim to none.

They could be wrong…

Morgan clambered to her feet, pulse pounding in her ears. She splashed cold water on her face, then brushed her teeth again before returning to the living room and slumping down on the couch, running through dates in her mind. It had been three weeks since she'd been with Ely on the beach. Early still, but an at-home test could be accurate.

What if I am pregnant?

A tiny frisson of excitement sparkled

through her before a second frisson of fear followed.

Even if she had somehow conceived, having a viable pregnancy was a long shot at best. With a history of ectopic pregnancy, she was at greater risk for another.

She took a deep breath, then exhaled, struggling to slow her racing pulse. More likely it *was* stress throwing off her cycle. That wasn't uncommon, and Lord knew she'd been under enough of it here on the island. No need to worry. She'd leave here tomorrow night, and her period would probably start right up again.

Then a sudden image of her holding a baby with Ely's dark hair and her blue eyes flashed into Morgan's mind, and she couldn't breathe. Couldn't do anything except cry. She wanted a family of her own more than anything, and the thought of that family including Ely and Dylan and a new baby seemed too perfect to be real. But she couldn't get her hopes up. Not yet. If by some miracle she was pregnant, it was still too early yet. She could still lose it. Or it could turn out to be ectopic again. And if that happened...

No.

Think logically. Take things slow.

First, confirm if she was even pregnant.

That meant a drive into the pharmacy at Langley for an over-the-counter test. Morgan slipped her feet into her sneakers before grabbing the keys to the sedan and her purse. Do the test. Then at least she'd know, one way or another.

That evening, Ely fiddled with the tricorn hat of his pirate ensemble. Dylan stood watching him, eyes round with wonder. He was dressed as a battle droid from the latest sci-fi flick and looked more adorable than intimidating, but Ely wasn't going to be the one to tell him.

"Are you excited to go to the ball tonight?" Ely asked his son.

"Yes! Mommy said I can have all the candy I want," Dylan said from the doorway.

Ely didn't buy that for a second, but he let it pass. There'd be plenty of people at the party to keep an eye on Dylan's sugar bingeing, including Morgan.

Morgan.

With a sigh, Ely stared at his reflection. He looked ridiculous with his fake sword and a stuffed parrot on his shoulder. He felt even worse, but that had nothing to do with his costume and everything to do with that last awful conversation with Morgan. They'd avoided each other after that night, and with his busy schedule he hadn't had the time or the mental wherewithal to confront her again. And while it wasn't entirely true, that was the excuse he was going with anyway.

Honestly, he didn't know what to say, really. Didn't know how to just put himself out there and risk it all to be with her. No matter how much he might love her and want to be with her. Knowing he was doing the right thing didn't stop his stubborn mind from remembering her laugh, her smile, the way her lovely eyes lit up when they'd been out sailing, the way she smelled like sunshine and flowers and hope. So much hope. Hope for a different future, a different life, one filled with family and love and laughter.

All the things he wanted. All the things slipping through his fingers after tonight.

"Ely? Are you in here?" Raina called, walking into the room. She stopped short at the sight of his getup. "Wow. Maybe I should've said, 'Argh, matey.'"

"Ha-ha," Ely said. "Not."

She was dressed in a gown that would've made Marie Antoinette jealous, her long blond hair twisted into a sophisticated-looking arrangement atop her head and a pair of diamond earrings he'd given her as a wedding gift twinkling in her ears. In her hand was the matching necklace. She held it out to him now. "Can you help me clasp this, please?"

Raina turned her back to him, and he quickly fastened it around her neck.

"Dylan, sweetie," she said to their son, "can you go check on Uncle Sam, please? See if he needs anything?"

The boy ran from the room, eager to help, as Raina faced Ely once more. "Want to tell me what's bothering you?"

"Nothing." Ely scowled down at his shiny black boots. "I'm fine. Why?"

She shook her head. "Because you're walking around like someone kicked your puppy."

"I most certainly am not." He looked past her into the mirror again, adjusting his parrot. Okay. Fine. Maybe he did look a little mopey. He had a black hole where his heart used to be. He was entitled to some wallowing.

Raina watched him, arms crossed and a brow raised. "You love her, don't you?"

Ely tried to play it off with a dismissive wave. "I don't know what you're talking about."

"Don't lie to me, Ely. I always know. It's a mom thing." She sat down on the edge of his bed with the regal air of the queen she was dressed like. "It's obvious, you know. The way you look at her. Like she's your favorite Christmas gift, the present you've always wanted."

He snorted. "Morgan and I are friends. Work colleagues. That's all."

Raina snorted. "Right. Sure."

Ely met her gaze in the mirror and frowned. "It doesn't matter what I feel, anyway. She's leaving tomorrow night, and that's the end of it."

"Did you tell her?"

"No." He tugged at his coat again, even though it was fine. "Why would I do that?"

"Because she has a right to know, Ely." Raina stared at him in the mirror, speaking slowly like he needed the extra time to absorb her words. Maybe he did. "I wish you'd learn that love isn't something any of us can control. Not you. Not anyone. It's wild and free, and that's the beauty of it. Love is a gift, Ely. And rather than accept it and cherish it, you think it's something to be feared and locked away."

She picked at the pale duvet beneath her fingers. "Losing someone you love is better than never having them in your life at all. Don't miss your opportunity to change, Ely. Talk to Morgan. Dylan loves her. You obviously do, too. Ask her what she wants, how she feels. Ask her to stay. Maybe she'll surprise you. Think about it. Just because things didn't work between us doesn't mean Morgan's not your perfect match. Take a risk. That's the only way you'll know." Raina stood and walked to the door. "The guests will be here soon. Meet you downstairs in five minutes."

CHAPTER FOURTEEN

BY SIX THAT NIGHT, Morgan had that deer-in-the-headlights look, shocked and scared and stunned out of her wits. The test sat there on the bathroom counter, two pink lines glowing cheerfully up at her, even though she still couldn't quite believe it.

Pregnant. I'm pregnant.

On autopilot, she dried her hair, then got dressed, shimmying into her mermaid costume without really paying much attention. She still wasn't keen on attending the ball, and the thought of seeing Ely right now made her feel sick all over again. Morgan absently placed a hand on her lower abdomen, wondering how he'd react, knowing she was carrying his baby.

Not that she'd mention it tonight. Not after what had happened last time. And the last thing she wanted was for him to be with her out of some misguided sense of responsibility. She'd had more than enough of that with Ben, thanks so much.

Of course, she'd never really thought about being a single mother, either. She'd never expected to be a mother at all, honestly. But life had a way of surprising you. And even though she'd just found out, even though the embryo couldn't have been more than the size of a poppy seed, she already loved her baby fiercely.

Morgan took a deep breath and straightened her dress. Her boobs were kind of sore, too, and from the online research she'd done earlier, that wasn't uncommon, even this early in gestation. Her smile grew until she was grinning like an idiot. Couldn't stop. For the first time in a long time, she finally felt like she had a future to look forward to.

So, fine. Enough feeling sorry for herself. She'd go to the ball, if only to make an appearance. Show Ely she was more than capable of thriving on her own. And when the time came, when she knew for certain the pregnancy would go to term, she'd tell him about their baby. Let him decide how he wanted to proceed at that point. If he wanted to stay in their lives, great. If not, they'd be okay, too.

She left her hair long and draped over one

shoulder, then applied shimmering green eye makeup and a final slick of gloss. There. Done. Ready to face whatever the evening threw at her.

Jeremy knocked on the door, right on time.

"Your carriage awaits," he joked when Morgan opened the door, her tail draped over one arm.

"Wow. You look amazing, Jeremy." He did, too. His hair was slicked back, and his Jedi robes looked like they'd come right off the movie set. He even had a trusty lightsaber at his side. "Is that your weapon or are you happy to see me?"

"Both?" Jeremy chuckled and walked into the cottage, shutting the door behind him. "And don't you look stunning, Princess of the Sea?"

"Thanks." According to the clock on the wall in the kitchen they still had a few minutes before they needed to leave, so they took a seat in the living room. "Can I get you something to drink?" Morgan asked. "Maybe some wine to take the edge off before the party?"

"Wine is always welcome." Jeremy relaxed back into the sofa cushions. "This is the first quiet moment to myself I think I've had all day. Don't think I've sat down, either, since I was here earlier."

"What's Gina going to be tonight?" Morgan poured him a glass of white wine, then got a sparkling water for herself before carrying both drinks back into the living room. "Was it a witch?"

"Fairy princess," he said, then raised a brow at her glass. "You're not having wine, too?"

"Uh, no," Morgan said. "I'm not much of a drinker."

They sipped in companionable silence for a few minutes.

"I almost wish we didn't have to go," Jeremy said at last. "Would be nice to just have a night in."

"Don't tempt me. You know how I felt earlier."

"Better now?" She nodded. Jeremy set his empty wineglass aside. "Good. Mind if I use your bathroom before we go?"

"Not at all."

A few minutes later, Jeremy returned, his expression curious as he held up the pregnancy test. *Crap.* She hadn't even thought about hiding it. Add brain fog to her list of symptoms.

"Is there something you want to tell me?"

He looked at the stick again. "I wasn't snooping, I swear. It was just sitting there on the counter, so… It's positive, right?"

For a moment, Morgan considered lying, but Jeremy was her friend, and she could really use a confidant right now. "Yes, it's positive. But you can't say a word to anyone."

"I swear." He sat beside her on the sofa again. "You don't look like this is good news."

She gave him a quick history of her previous pregnancy. "I honestly didn't think it was possible. All the doctors told me the chances of it happening again were basically nil after last time, but I guess they were wrong."

"Wow." Jeremy took her hand, his expression concerned. "Is this good news, then?"

Morgan stood and took the stick from him, frowning. "I don't know. Yes, I mean, I'm happy about the baby. But I'm also scared. I don't want to get too excited yet, because it's still early and there's a chance it could be another ectopic pregnancy, which would not be good, so…"

"When will you know?" He lowered his voice. "More importantly, who's the father?"

Morgan's cheeks prickled with heat, and Jeremy gaped.

"Oh, my God! It's Ely's? Have you told him yet?"

"No. And that's why you can't say anything to anyone, understand? Not Ely, not Sam, not Raina. Not even Gina or Dylan. No one." She walked the pregnancy test back to the bathroom, then returned. "I'm going to tell Ely, eventually. Once I know for certain the pregnancy is viable, then—and only then—will I say a word to him about it."

Jeremy's smile fell. "Oh, Morgan. I really think you should tell him now. He should know. And if there are complications, he can be there for you, by your side. You shouldn't have to go through this alone."

"No." Morgan bit her lip. "I don't want him to feel like he needs to be with me just because of the baby. I want a man by my side who's there because he loves me, not out of some sense of obligation." Her voice shook despite her wishes. "And what if this pregnancy isn't viable?" She shook her head, blinking back tears. "No. I can't do that to him. I'm sorry, Jeremy, but you need to let me do this my way, okay?"

"Okay." He exhaled slow. "I won't say anything. Promise."

"Good." Morgan started toward the door. "Now, let's get going to this ball."

By the time they arrived at Wingate, the gala was in full swing. Morgan thought she recognized several faces behind the masks and makeup—a few patients and most of the staff as well. A wide variety of costumes filled the house, everything from superheroes to animals and even a few inanimate objects like dice and power tools. Spooky music filled the air, and the estate was decorated to the hilt with a corn maze set up outside for the kids, lots of black lights and spiderwebs and jack-o'-lanterns. Skeletons occupied many a corner, and ghoulish green garlands of strung-together bones surrounded the banisters in the foyer.

A small local band was set up in one room, along with a dance floor, and were cranking out "Monster Mash" at earsplitting levels. Everything was all so festive and fun, and soon Morgan found her cares and worries disappearing, her toes tapping to the lively beat. Through the throng of guests, she spotted Ely across the room, dressed as a pirate with Raina beside him, looking resplendent in a courtesan costume. They certainly made a striking pair, tall and gorgeous.

Ely's head was bent toward another guest as he listened to what they were saying. It wasn't until the crowd parted slightly that Morgan saw it was Dr. Greg and Peggy he was speaking to. Excited to hear all about their trip, Morgan headed over, too, despite her plans to avoid Ely as much as possible. As she approached, her gaze locked with Ely's, and for a moment the rest of the world fell away.

Morgan looked anywhere but at him as she greeted Dr. Greg and Peggy.

"Welcome, Dr. Salas." Raina hugged her. "You look amazing. I always wanted to be a mermaid."

"Sounds like things have been pretty exciting at the clinic since I left, Morgan," Dr. Greg said, picking up the thread of conversation and running with it. "Sea rescues, emergency surgeries. Ely says you handled it all like a pro, though."

"I did my best." She smiled. "It's wonderful to have you back. How was Australia?"

"Beautiful." Peggy beamed. "We'll have you over for dinner tomorrow before you leave to tell you all about it. Ely, too. That way you can both catch my husband up to speed on his patients at the same time."

"Daddy!" Dylan ran up to them, colliding with his father's legs.

"Hey, buddy." Ely laughed, hugging his son around the shoulders. "Slow down."

"Sorry." The little boy looked up at Morgan. "Where've you been, Dr. Salas? When can we go sailing again?"

"Oh. Well, I think we'll have to take a rain check on that, since I'm leaving tomorrow night." The words hurt more than she expected, and she swallowed hard around the lump in her throat.

"No!" Dylan said, transferring his embrace from Ely's legs to hers. "Don't go, Dr. Salas. I don't want you to leave. Please stay with me. You can live with Daddy and me and we'll all be happy ever after, just like the movies."

Her heart pinched, and Morgan's breath caught. Her gaze flew to Ely's, and he looked as uncomfortable as she felt.

"You know," Raina said, coming to her rescue and pulling Dylan to her side, "I never got a chance to thank you, Morgan, for all you did for my son. If anything had happened to Dylan…" Her voice cracked a bit, and Morgan's chest ached even more. Without thinking, she placed her hand atop her abdomen again.

She looked down at the crying little boy, then crouched in front of him. "Even if I'm gone, you can still call me, you know. I'll give you my number. Anytime, day or night, I'll be here for you, whenever you need me."

Dylan sighed, his cheeks damp and red. "I

love you, Dr. Salas. You made me all better."
He hugged her tight, burying his face in her
neck, and Morgan closed her eyes, soaking it
all in, saving it to comfort her later. "You look
really pretty, Dr. Salas," Dylan said at last,
leaning back slightly to look at her. "Don't
you think she looks pretty, Daddy? You
should tell her she looks pretty, too, Daddy,
so she isn't so sad."

Oh, boy.

The last thing Morgan wanted was to cry
in front of everyone. She straightened then,
smoothing her hand down the front of her
shimmering green dress. She could feel the
eyes of the group on her, and her stomach
lurched. She shouldn't have come tonight
after all, especially with her hormones out of
whack. It was too much. It was all too much.
"Uh, please excuse me. I need some air. Dr.
Greg, Peggy, so glad to have you back. Can't
wait to hear about your trip tomorrow."

Morgan walked away as dignified as she
could with her mermaid tail draped over her
arm, aware of people glancing her way. She
didn't stop until she found Jeremy standing
near the buffet tables, eyeing the caterers'
setup critically. Every conceivable kind of
hors d'oeuvre and finger food seemed to be
there—bowls of shrimp and platters of meat

and cheese and crudités, even tiny cakes decorated with swirls of chocolate and cream. If her stomach hadn't been in knots, she might have tried some.

"I'm not sure there's enough," Jeremy said, his tone anxious. "Do you think there's enough?"

"You're kidding, right?" Morgan gave him an incredulous look. "There's enough stuff to feed the entire island twice over."

"Well, I guess that's good, because it looks like most of the island is here," Jeremy said. "I haven't seen a party at Wingate so heavily attended since New Year's Eve. Lots of people come to the island just for that event each year." He looked at Morgan. "Maybe you'll even be here for it, eh?"

No. She wouldn't. Morgan stared at her toes. It was best if she left. Went to see her parents, took some time to figure out where her life would go from here. Start over fresh somewhere new. It would be hard leaving Whidbey Island, though, especially since she was just starting to feel like she belonged there, but it wasn't the end of the world. She couldn't let it be.

"Hey." Jeremy put his hand on Morgan's shoulder. "Everything will work out. You'll see."

Before she could respond, a tall, dark-haired man joined them. He was slimmer and a bit shorter than Ely, but there was no mistaking the resemblance.

"There you are, Jeremy," the man said, slipping an arm around Jeremy's waist and pulling him close. "I've been looking for you everywhere. Don't tell me you're worrying about the food. This is your night off."

"Sam, let me introduce you to Dr. Salas," Jeremy said, ignoring his other statements. "Morgan, this is Ely's younger brother, Samuel Malik."

"So nice to finally meet you, Dr. Salas." He smiled, then bent to kiss her hand, a charmer for sure. Something else the Malik brothers shared, apparently. In the background, the band was halfway through a rousing rendition of "Don't Fear the Reaper." Sam grinned, looking between her and Jeremy. "What do you say we all hit the dance floor and get our groove on?"

"Uh…" Out of the corner of her eye, she saw Dr. Greg and Peggy talking to Raina, but Ely wasn't with them anymore. His location soon became apparent, though, when someone tapped on her shoulder and she turned to find Ely blocking her path.

"May I have the next dance?" he asked, holding out a hand to her.

The band started a lovely, slow rendition of "Zombie" by the Cranberries, and Morgan didn't want to make a scene, dammit, so she accepted. They walked to the dance floor, and Morgan did her best to relax in his arms as they swayed to the music, her tail draped over her arm and his fake parrot bobbing on his shoulder, but it was difficult.

"Okay?" he asked as more couples joined them.

"Fine." But between the warm, gentle pressure of his hand on her lower back and the brush of his body against hers, she felt like a complete mess inside. To make matters worse, the thought that this could be their one and only dance together made her eyes sting once more with unshed tears.

No. No, no, no. Stop it.

She would not cry here. She wouldn't.

"Penny for your thoughts?" he whispered near her ear, making her shiver.

Morgan sighed, then looked up at him. "I'm thinking about leaving."

She felt his intake of breath.

He glanced around before maneuvering her toward an open door that led out to the empty patio. A breeze blew, cooling her overheated skin and making her shiver. Ely slipped off his pirate coat and wrapped it around her shoulders, leaving him in his frilly white shirt and black pants, like some historical romance novel cover model. His arm brushed hers as he leaned on the railing, and her heart hurt even worse. For all they'd had and all they'd lost.

"I thought you should know." His quiet voice filled the darkness. Her breath caught, held. "Dr. Greg's going to ask you to stay. For the record, I told him I think you'll make an excellent addition to the practice." Ely gave a tentative smile. "We'd be lucky to have you."

Well, damn. Not what she'd hoped to hear from him. A job offer wasn't bad, but she couldn't take it. Working with Ely every day, knowing he wasn't hers, would never be hers, would be too hard. And what about the baby? Hard to hide that once she started showing. Her throat dried, and she swallowed hard. "I, uh… I don't know. Won't that be awkward? Us working together, after what happened?"

The breeze blew again, harder this time. Through the soft, dim light filtering out through the open doors behind them, Ely looked…broken, somehow. Vulnerable. She'd never seen that in him before.

"What I said that night, Morgan… Not just

about staying. About everything. Or what I didn't say." He shook his head then sighed, his broad shoulders slumping. "I wish you didn't have to go." The words were so soft, she would've missed them if she hadn't been paying attention. Then he turned slightly and touched her hair, pain lurking in his tawny eyes. "I wish…"

"What?" she whispered, the rush of blood in her ears drowning out everything but him. "What do you wish?"

His fingers traced down her cheek to her jaw. "I wish I'd called you all those years ago."

They both gave a short laugh, then stilled. Time slowed as Ely kissed her again. Morgan froze at first, then melted against him. His pirate coat fell from her shoulders and hit the ground as the kiss turned hungry, desperate, until finally Ely pulled back, their ragged breaths the only sound in the otherwise quiet night. "God, Morgan. I want you so much."

"I know," she said, summoning every ounce of willpower she had to push him away. "But that's not enough."

The sound of a clearing throat had them both looking at the door again. "Sorry to interrupt," Raina said. "But Jeremy's looking for you, Ely. A problem with the caterers or something."

Morgan stepped back and nearly tripped over her tail, which had fallen from her arm during her kiss with Ely. She scooped it up now, embarrassed and just wanting to go home and have a good cry. "I'm actually going to head back to the cottage, I think. Lots of packing to do before tomorrow. Excuse me."

Behind her, Ely said, "Morgan, wait…"

But she was already gone, back into the stuffy house, where too many people in too many costumes were pressed together like sardines. Except now she remembered that Jeremy had driven her over. Damn. As she neared the buffet tables again, she saw him and Sam talking, their heads bowed together, each giving the other heart-eyed looks. Good. She was happy for them. Jeremy deserved his happily-ever-after. At least one of them would get it. She couldn't ask him to leave the party now, but maybe he'd let her drive his car back to the cottage, then she could bring it back tomorrow.

Yes. That sounded good. The rain from earlier had stopped, so it should be an easy drive. She'd walk, but it was night, and the last thing she needed now was to get lost again.

She approached the two men, then waited for a them to notice her so as not to interrupt anything. "So sorry, Jeremy," she said with faux brightness. "But I've just remembered something important I need to do back at the cottage."

Like sob myself to sleep in my pillow.

"Would it be a problem if I drove your car there, then brought it back in the morning?"

Jeremy's gaze narrowed. "Everything okay?"

"Yes, fine," she said too fast, her chest tight. "I just have so much to do before I leave. I've made my rounds here, so now I'd just really like to get back to it."

"I'll take you." Jeremy set his sparkling water aside.

"No, no." Morgan held up a hand in protest, glancing at Sam. "Seriously. I'll be fine. It's not far, and you two are having such a good time, I don't want to break that up."

Jeremy exchanged a look with Sam before sighing and slipping the keys out of his Jedi robes. "Fine. But call me once you get there so I know you made it okay. And please be careful."

"Always," she said, relieved beyond measure. "So nice to finally meet you, Sam."

"Same." They hugged briefly, then she was

off to the front entrance, heart racing in time with the steps, hurrying through the crowd like the hounds of hell were after her, because it kind of felt like they were. All the ghosts of her past, all her mistakes, all her missed opportunities, haunting her tonight.

She found Jeremy's car and climbed in behind the wheel, cramming her mermaid tail into the passenger seat, then started the engine. The costume restricted her leg movements, which made working the pedals more difficult, which was why she'd ridden with Jeremy to begin with, but it was too late now. She'd make do. After adjusting her mirrors and fastening her seat belt, she eased out of the parking spot and started down the drive to the main roadway. The sky was dotted with clouds, but the moon peeked through now and again. Between that and her headlights, she could see well enough, though the area looked different at night. Lots of odd shapes and sinister shadows. Very fitting for Halloween.

At the bottom of the hill, she turned out on the roadway, heading for the cottage. Images from the day replayed in her mind like a movie. Being ill that morning. The positive pregnancy test. Telling Jeremy. Arriving at the party. Kissing Ely goodbye on the patio.

That last one stabbed her hard between the

ribs. God, she was going to miss him. Dylan, too. And Jeremy. There was so much she was going to miss about Whidbey Island. But she couldn't stay, not with the way things were now.

Ahead, something streaked across the headlight beams, glaring white. An animal, maybe? Morgan slammed on the brakes, and the car skidded. The road was still damp, and before she knew what was happening, the back end fishtailed off the asphalt and onto the muddy berm. From there it was a slow slide into the ditch on the other side.

Perfect. Right back where she'd started.

Grumbling, Morgan gunned the engine like she'd seen Ely do that first day, but it didn't work. Just sent mud flying everywhere. Next, she got her door open and crawled out, only to end up on her butt on the ground because her tail got caught between the car interior and the door. She fell awkwardly with her ankle beneath her, and pain shot up her leg. Dammit. She wiggled the toes, and luckily, they still seemed to be working. Each tiny movement sent bolts of agony through her nervous system, though. Tried to stand on it, but nope. Wouldn't support any weight. She collapsed back down in the mud as a distant *baa* echoed on the air.

Foiled by sheep. Again.

Cursing, she took a deep breath, then reached into her shell-covered bra top for her cell phone. She turned it on, but of course there was no service out here. Perfect.

Above her, on the roadway, she heard cars pass, but no one could see her down here in the ditch. The engine was still running, though, so maybe she could use the hazard lights to signal for help. Except that would mean moving, and moving was nearly impossible with her sore ankle.

Still, she had to try. For herself. For the baby.

Slowly, excruciatingly, inch by inch, she managed to get to her knees, then hauled her upper body back through the open car door and strained to reach the hazard light button on the dashboard.

Click.

Then, exhausted, she flopped back onto her butt to wait. Wait and pray someone would find her soon before she froze to death out here.

CHAPTER FIFTEEN

ELY STOOD FOR a long moment after Morgan walked away, feeling like his entire world had imploded. Then, oddly numb, he bent to pick up his coat from the ground where it had fallen before looking at Raina. "You were right. I do love Morgan. But I can't ask her to stay here when she wants to go."

His ex-wife crossed her arms, tapping her slipper-covered toe impatiently on the flagstones. "Did you even ask her?"

"No," he said, pulling his coat back on, the stuffed bird sitting crookedly now, but Ely didn't care. "But I did tell her Dr. Greg was going to offer her a permanent position at the clinic. If she'd wanted to stay here, that should've changed her mind. It didn't."

"Men," Raina muttered, walking over to him to adjust his parrot. "She doesn't care about the job. Okay. Scratch that. She does care about the job. Very much. But she also cares about you, Ely." She stepped back and sighed, hands on her hips. "Look. I know you're a control freak. Lord knows I lived with it long enough. And I know you want everything to be certain. But that's not how life works, Ely. Sometimes you have to have to jump first, then look later. Otherwise, you're just going to resign yourself to being miserable the rest of your life.

"Seriously, Ely. You need to give Morgan a reason to stay besides the job. Give her your heart. Let her know how you feel, how important she is to you. There's no guarantee, but I'd bet good money she feels the same. And maybe, if she knew how you felt, that might make all the difference. I know you, Ely Malik. Don't you dare go comparing what happened with us to what's going on between you and Morgan. Don't. Everyone wants different things, and that's great. It's what makes the world such an interesting place. I love my job and it requires me to travel a lot and I'm okay with that. But Morgan doesn't strike me as someone stricken with wanderlust. Just the opposite. So, go find her and proclaim your love. I'll bet good money you sweep her off her feet before the night is through."

Ely wasn't a man who liked to gamble, especially with his heart, but deep down he knew he had to try. He'd let Morgan get away once in his life. Fate was giving him another shot, and he didn't want to lose her again. It had been a long, hard road to get here. But he'd gotten clear, finally.

Because of Morgan.

"Okay. I will." He squared his shoulders, pulled his tricorn hat lower, then headed inside.

The crowd parted before him as he made a beeline toward the buffet table, thinking maybe Morgan had gone back to Jeremy and Sam. But when he got there, she wasn't with them.

"Have you seen Morgan?" Ely glanced around the room. "I was just with her on the patio."

"No," Jeremy said. "She left. Took my car keys to drive herself back to the cottage."

Dammit. He didn't like her being out alone at night. "And you let her go?"

"I offered to drive her myself, but she said she'd make it fine on her own." Jeremy frowned. "Why? What happened, Ely? Is everything okay?"

"No. Everything definitely is not okay." He stalked off toward the foyer, running into Mrs. MacIntosh, who was dressed like the teapot from *Beauty and the Beast*. He snagged his housekeeper by the handle. "Did you see Dr. Salas leave? How long ago was it?"

"Yes," she said, her nod making her lid hat wobble on her head. "About five minutes ago. Said she was going back to the cottage."

Ely hurried outside. Maybe Morgan was still making her way through the maze of cars out front, but no. Beyond the lighting around the house, it was pitch-dark. Unease bored into his belly. He found his truck and climbed in, heading down the drive.

By the time he reached the main road, he had to turn on his bright beams to see any distance in front of him, and worry sprouted tentacles and wormed through his body. The island might be close to Seattle, but it felt like a world away out here. Occasionally the moon peeked out from behind the clouds, illuminating the land on either side of him. He had the window down and despite the cool night air slapping his face, his skin burned and his pulse raced.

God, why didn't I just tell her I loved her and beg her to stay?

That would've been so easy. But no. He'd had to keep it all inside, just like always. Growing up too soon, it had been a defense mechanism, a way to protect himself. Now, it was just keeping him away from the thing he wanted most in the world. His feet ached in his shiny pirate boots, but that was the least of his concerns. He had to find Morgan. Had to tell her how he felt. Had to beg her forgiveness.

Halfway to the cottage, a brief flash from somewhere below the road to his right made him slow down, then back up, after checking to make sure there were no cars coming behind him. Ely eased onto the berm and put the car in Park, took a couple deep steadying breaths. *Calm down.* He needed to calm down and think. He'd lived here all his life. Used to play on this land as a kid. There'd been a time when he could find his way to the cottage and back blindfolded. Chances were good that Morgan was already home and he was making a big deal out of nothing. Still, he couldn't seem to shake the feeling that something was wrong...

Then, there. Again.

Another flash, from below the edge of the berm, fainter this time. He cut the engine and got out. The moon had completely disappeared behind the clouds now, and from the scent of the air, it would probably rain again soon. If Morgan was still out here, he needed to find her. Ely pulled out his phone and turned on the flashlight app, only to see his battery was nearly dead. Not good. And even if he wanted to call someone to help him search, there was no signal.

Just keep going. Keep moving. Morgan needs you.

In the stillness, waves crashed against the distant shore. Keeping the water to his right, he continued to search, sweeping his phone in front of him from side to side in case Morgan was lying on the ground somewhere, hurt or bleeding. Images of the plane crash that killed his parents flickered in his head—the carnage, the destruction, the death—and they robbed the oxygen from his lungs making him breathe harder. Morgan had been lucky that first day on the island. He'd been there to rescue her then. If he had his way, he'd always be there to rescue her.

Please, God, let her be okay. Must find her. Have to find her.

He hadn't been able to save his parents, but maybe, just maybe, he could save Morgan.

Then a sound. Faint at first, carried on the wind. He stopped and listened.

A voice. Someone calling for help. He headed down the embankment toward the noise, barely making out a huddled figure on the ground at the bottom of the ditch. The closer he got, the more an outline emerged. A woman, with a mermaid tail. Morgan. He'd found Morgan.

Heart slamming against his rib cage, he moved slowly toward her over the craggy rocks. Then she cried out and he threw caution to the wind, leaping and jumping and running, running for her and calling her name, not caring about the mud sucking at his boots or the slippery rocks or the fact he'd probably have to buy this stupid costume now because of the damage. It didn't matter. Nothing mattered except the fact that she was safe. He sank to his knees in front of her and pulled her into his arms, his voice shaky and rough. "Are you all right? I was so worried. What happened?"

"I was heading back to the cottage and then something ran in front of the car. A sheep, I think," she said, wincing. "And I think my a-ankle's b-broken," she stammered, shaking so badly now it was hard make out her words. "S-stupid t-tail. G-got c-caught."

"Shh." He held her closer, kissing her hair, breathing her in. "I've got you. I've got you. I won't let you go. I won't ever let you go."

Morgan went quiet then. Either she'd

fainted or fallen asleep. Regardless, he needed to get her inside and warmed up. Ely carefully picked her up and carried her up the embankment to his truck, then drove her to the cottage. He'd send a tow truck to retrieve Jeremy's car in the morning. For now, his top priority was Morgan.

Once inside, he laid her on the sofa and covered her with a blanket, then rekindled the fire. After the flames were crackling again, he returned to her side and knelt on the floor, slipping off her shoes, then taking one of her chilled hands in his. "Just rest, *janaan*. I'll stay here with you."

She peeked one bleary eye open and whispered groggily, "Still don't know what that means."

"Beloved." Ely smiled and kissed her fingers. "Because that's what you are. My beloved."

Her smile lit up his night before she drifted off again.

Ely made sure she was warming up, then examined her ankle. Swollen and bruised, but from what he could tell, at that point, at least, not broken. He'd tape it up now, then drive her to the clinic in the morning to get it x-rayed to be sure. Ely went in search of her medical kit for supplies.

* * *

Morgan awoke from a deep, dreamless sleep and opened her eyes to find dawn breaking through the windows of the cottage. Ely sat across from her, still wearing his frilly shirt and tight black pants from the night before. She blinked a few times to make sure she wasn't imagining him, then tried to move her sore ankle, but it was taped too tight. Ely must've taken care of it while she'd slept.

"Good morning," he said, watching her over his steepled fingers. "How are you feeling?"

Morgan frowned, her head fuzzy as she mumbled, "Sore. Is my ankle broken?"

"I don't think so, but we'll check at the clinic later anyway. Probably still hurts, though."

"It does." She tried to sit up, then winced. He came around to help her, getting her comfortably snuggled into the pillows in the corner before taking a seat at the other end of the sofa. Morgan looked down to find she was still in her costume as well. Great. She must look like a real horror show this morning. How fitting for the season. "How'd you find me last night? Did you see my hazard lights?"

"Sort of. I saw some brief flashes from the side of the road, but nothing I could really follow. I'm pretty sure Jeremy needs a new battery in his car now." Ely huffed out a breath and sat forward, burying his hands in his hair. "God, Morgan, what the hell were you thinking? You know what the terrain is like around here. You scared me half to death, wandering off like that at night."

"Sorry." She adjusted her weight, then sighed. "Did you sit here all night with me? What about your party?"

"It's fine. And I don't give a damn about the party. I'm sure it went fine without me." He looked over at her, and just like that, her heart tumbled, the same way it had each time she'd seen him since that very first night all those years ago, the same connection that drew her back to Ely like a moth to a flame and kept her in thrall. She'd always return to him, she realized now. Because he was her person. Ely Malik was the one. And no amount of hiding or running away would change that. Not now. Not ever.

"The only thing I cared about last night was you, Morgan," he continued: "And I'm sorry I didn't say it sooner. I should have, but I was scared." He huffed out a breath, staring at the floor between his knees. "God, I've been such an idiot this past month, trying to control everything, acting like keeping you away would protect me, protect the life I'd built here for Dylan and me. But it was too late. That life changed the minute you set foot on this island. I changed. I'm not the same man I was a month ago, Morgan, and I have you to thank for that. I care for you so much it hurts. I love you, Morgan Salas. Always will."

Her stomach flipped with happiness this time, her pulse trilling like chimes in the wind. "You love me?"

"Yes. God, yes. I love you! I don't go around calling just anyone my beloved." He shook his head, and his hands dangled limply between his knees now as he flashed a rueful smile. "After I got a stern talking-to from Raina, I went inside to talk to you, to tell you how I felt. But then Jeremy said you'd left and…" He scrubbed a hand over his weary face. He still looked wonderful to her, maybe even more so all scruffy and tousled. "I went after you. I was scared out of my wits. Especially knowing how cold it gets at night and how dark. God, if I hadn't found you, Morgan, you could be dead out there."

His voice broke, and she moved then despite the pain, unable to resist hugging him. "But you did find me."

"I'll always find you, Morgan." He turned

and kissed her, soft and sweet and gentle. "I lost you once. I never want to lose you again."

She sighed and rested her forehead against his. There were still things he didn't know. Important things. Maybe the most important thing. Morgan took a deep breath and said, "I'm pregnant."

For a long moment, Ely just blinked at her. "I'm sorry. What?"

Morgan swallowed hard, uncertainty threatening to overwhelm her. But no. This was Ely. She trusted Ely. She always would. "I didn't think it could happen again. The doctors told me it couldn't. But I guess they were wrong. I'd been feeling sick in the mornings for a while, and at first I thought it was the flu, but then my period was late this month and I'm always like clockwork, so I went into town yesterday and bought a pregnancy test, and it was positive, and—"

She didn't get to say anything else then, because Ely was kissing her again, pulling her into his arms, her blanket falling to her waist. When he finally pulled back, he was grinning from ear to ear.

Her heart stumbled. "Please don't get too excited yet. It's still early and things could go wrong. With my history of ectopic pregnancy, I'll be high-risk either way." Morgan sighed. "I wasn't going to tell you until I was sure the pregnancy was viable."

"Ah, Morgan," he said, kissing her once more before snuggling in beside her. "I know there are still risks, but I don't care. We'll make an appointment at Seattle General for a full workup. And no matter what happens, we're still a family. You, me and Dylan."

"Don't forget Jeremy and Sam, too. Even Raina. Maybe even Dr. Greg and Peggy." Morgan settled in, letting the warmth of the fire and Ely seep into her tired bones. For the first time since the previous morning she was relaxing at last. Maybe they didn't have it all figured out. Maybe they both still had doubts. But one thing she'd never doubt was Ely. He'd more than proven to her during her time here that he was trustworthy. After all the pain Ben had caused her, she could let someone in again.

Let Ely in again.

"You're right," she said finally. "I don't want to waste this second chance we've gotten, either. I love you so much."

"And I love you, Morgan," he murmured against her temple. "I want to grow old with you, side by side. We're meant to be together. We've already wasted enough years." Ely met her gaze, his tawny eyes bright with honesty. "Let's not waste any more time. Please."

"I love Dylan, too, you know," Morgan said. "He's like my own son."

"Dylan loves you back. He'll be thrilled to have you with us at Wingate. He said as much earlier, after all. So much wiser than us."

She smiled. "Yep. Smart kid."

"He really is." Ely gave her a squeeze. "So, will you marry me, Morgan?"

It would be so easy to say yes right now. She wanted nothing more than to spend the rest of her life with him. But she didn't want to rush it. If something happened with the baby and he changed his mind about her like Ben had, it would break her heart.

"Give me a little time. Okay? I'm not going anywhere."

He leaned up to meet her gaze. "You're not?"

"Nope." Morgan grinned, not realizing until right then that she meant it. "I'm not. Can't go turning down Dr. Greg's offer, now can I?"

EPILOGUE

Ten months later

Morgan sat by a crackling fire in the nursery she and Ely had painstakingly decorated at Wingate, nursing newborn Ari—short for Arham, after Ely's father. The baby's blue eyes, just like his momma's, slowly drifted closed, and a wave of complete contentment washed over her.

Despite a few bumps in the road, she'd carried the baby to full term. Had been on bed rest for the last six weeks of the pregnancy, which made everyone cranky, but she'd do it all again in a heartbeat.

"Hey," Ely said from the doorway, tiptoeing over quietly to crouch beside her chair, stroking his son's downy head. He'd put Dylan to bed, and finally the never-ending stream of guests and well-wishers over the last few weeks had subsided. She loved the sense of community on the island, but Morgan was exhausted and planned to go to sleep herself just as soon as she got Ari down for the night.

Ely looked tired, too, his hair a mess, dark circles under his eyes, a shadow of stubble on his jaw. He was still the most gorgeous man she'd ever seen. He grinned back, shifting slightly to pull something from the pocket of his black sweats. It took her a moment to realize it was a ring box. Frowning, Morgan glanced at him. "What's that?" They'd gotten so many gifts recently for the baby, but jewelry seemed a bit over-the-top. "Ari won't be old enough to wear that for a while yet."

"Good thing it's not for him then, huh?" Ely creaked the tiny velvet box open to reveal a beautiful antique diamond and sapphire ring. It sparkled in the firelight, or maybe that was the unexpected tears in her eyes. "Morgan Salas, love of my life, mother of my child. Will you please, finally, do me the honor of being my wife?"

She bit her lip, so choked up she could barely speak. "Oh, God. Yes. Yes, I'll marry you, Ely. Love of my life. Father of my child."

It had taken her nearly a year, and a lifetime of regrets, to reach this point. But now she was here, with Ely, with their family—the one they'd created together, from friends and those they cared for—and she never wanted to leave again. He slipped the ring on her finger, then kissed her.

"I love you, Morgan. Forever," he whispered, his forehead to hers in the firelight.

"I love you, too, Ely," she said. "Forever and ever, amen."

* * * * *

If you enjoyed this story, check out these other great reads from Traci Douglass

Costa Rican Fling with the Doc
Her One-Night Secret
The Vet's Unexpected Hero
Neurosurgeon's Christmas to Remember

All available now!